The room became so still that Bertram found it eerie. Then Poppa began to chant in a language Bertram had never heard before. He continued in English: "If there are any spirits present, let yourselves be known. Is Pygmalion Potter present? We are looking for Pygmalion Potter."

Suddenly there was a loud tapping on the door to Poppa's lab.

Bertram jumped. "Oh, no, it's my parents!" he cried with alarm.

"Come in," Poppa called in a loud, cheerful voice.

The tapping stopped instantly, and the door to the lab creaked open.

"Well," said a voice, "why do you look so surprised? Weren't you expecting me?"

Bertram instantly recognized the figure before him: It was Great-great-grandfather Pygmalion!

#2
Back To The Grave

Marc Gave

PRICE STERN SLOAN
Los Angeles

Produced by Cloverdale Press, Inc.
96 Morton Street
New York, New York 10014

Published by Price Stern Sloan, Inc.
360 North La Cienega Boulevard
Los Angeles, California 90048

ISBN: 0-8431-2711-2

10 9 8 7 6 5 4 3 2 1

— One —

Eleven-year-old Bertram Potter knew there was nowhere he would rather be on a chilly, rainy December evening than with his grandfather. That's why, after finishing his homework, Bertram, flashlight in hand, was scampering through the dark corridors of the Fear Factory, the wax museum his family owned. Poppa's apartment was tucked behind one corner of the museum, in the opposite corner from Bertram's own room on the second floor. Bertram knocked at Poppa's door using his special code, one long knock and three short knocks — which spelled the letter *B*, for Bertram, in Morse Code. Receiving no answer, Bertram waited a moment. Then he opened the door and walked in.

Making his way past the tiny kitchen into the living room, Bertram could see his grandfather through the open door of the lab. His glasses were perched on the end of his nose. The overhead light shone down on his partly bald head, from which tufts of untamed hair stuck out in all directions. Poppa was reading aloud to himself, as he often did. He claimed it helped him to remember what he read.

" 'And so, in conclusion, it is not only possible but actually quite simple to communicate with the spirit of the departed. Moreover, it is equally possible to conjure up an actual likeness of the living person. The conjurer should be able to make it stay until such time as he or she wishes to return the spirit to the life beyond.' "

"Is that book a joke, or what?" Bertram asked from the doorway.

Poppa turned around. "Bertram, my boy! You came just in time. No, this book is not a joke. It has wonderful things in it, serious things. In fact," he said with a wink, "it's *dead* serious."

Bertram grinned at Poppa. He thought he had read all of Poppa's magic books, but he had never seen this one before. It was small and had a faded bronze cover with elaborate, curvy designs. Bertram walked over to the stool where Poppa sat. He flipped to the title page. The book was called *The Babylonian Book of the Dead*. The author was Robertson Daniels, and it had been published in 1909 by Damon Publishers, London, England.

"I've never seen this book before, said Bertram. "You haven't been holding out on me, have you?"

"Would I do that?" said Poppa, pretending to be hurt. "I picked it up in a used-book store the last time I was in New Orleans. I just hadn't gotten around to looking at it before now. I wanted to check it out first in case it wasn't any good. But I think this is the real thing." He grinned. "I think it will come in very handy in the next few days." Bertram's eyes gleamed with excitement. "Does that mean you're planning to bring somebody back from the dead?" he asked.

Poppa nodded.

"Who do you have in mind?"

"Well, I thought you could help me decide. But the person *I'd* most like to see is my grandfather Pygmalion Potter. What a character! You know, he was the one who started the Potters on their road to fame and fortune in the wax museum business," Poppa explained.

"Let's see — that makes him my great-great-grandfather," said Bertram with pride. "Isn't he the one with the fancy cane in the picture in the upstairs hall?"

"Exactly," said Poppa. "It was the most beautiful cane in the whole town of Black Bayou, Louisiana. It had a real gold tip. Pygmalion was buried with it.

"I really miss the old fellow. I wish he had been around when I mixed up that batch of X-13 and made the statue walk. I can imagine

3

how much he would have enjoyed that."

X-13 was the name Poppa and Bertram had given to an old Egyptian recipe that Poppa had stumbled across in one of his magic books. Supposedly it had been used to make mummies walk. Poppa had tried painting some on one of the Fear Factory's wax statues, but nothing had happened. Then Bertram had poured some into the waxy mixture for a new statue, and it *had* come to life — much to their distress!

A horrible-looking creature known as "The Man Being Boiled Alive" had terrorized the town of Black Bayou for several days afterward. Bertram and Poppa stood to get into a mess of trouble if their mayor, Horace Q. Wright, found out. He and his group of friends in the Citizens for Decency group had already come close to shutting down the Fear Factory, several times in fact. But the walking statue had actually saved them.

"Why?" Bertram had said jokingly after they had finally caught The Man Being Boiled Alive. "Just because Horace went around trying to convince everybody that it wasn't a live monster but a statue *you* made walk? I wish I could have taken his picture when the members of the Citizens for Decency told him he'd been working too hard and handed him a plane ticket to Florida!"

"Yes, Pygmalion would have been proud of us

that day," said Poppa. "He would have seen I'm doing a fine job following in his footsteps. You see, Pygmalion had a rough time with Horace Q. Wright's granddaddy. He claimed he was trying to make peace with Silas Wright when he invited him to 'tour and tea,' but it kind of backfired."

"What happened?" Bertram asked.

"Well, to try to make peace between the Potters and the Wrights, Pygmalion invited Silas and his wife over for a special guided tour of the museum. That was to be followed by some light refreshment upstairs. But they never got to that. In those days the museum was closed on Sundays. Pygmalion's handyman, Alain, did repair work some Sundays in the museum.

"But I guess no one realized he was going to be working that Sunday. Pygmalion, your grandmother, Isabelle, and I were taking the Wrights through the museum. We came to one section that was entirely dark. We couldn't see a thing. No lights came on in the showcase to light up the exhibit, which was 'The Headless Horseman.'

"Laverne Wright said in a loud voice, 'Pygmalion, what's the meaning of this?' All of a sudden up pops Alain, and he flicks on a flashlight. Well, Laverne fainted dead away. We had to carry her upstairs and give her smelling salts. Alain had been sleeping, and

Laverne had woken him with her loud comment. It was a hoot, but we couldn't laugh.

"When Laverne came to, she and Silas got out of the house as quickly as they could. And that was the end of patching up differences between the Potters and the Wrights!"

"That's great!" said Bertram. "It sounds like something that would happen with the Wrights today. Do you have any more Pygmalion stories?"

"There was the time I helped him and Jessie Mae elope," said Poppa.

"Jessie Mae was Pygmalion's second wife, right?" said Bertram.

"That's right," Poppa answered. "Eugenie, Pygmalion's first wife, died after they had been married for sixty years. Grandma Eugenie was a wonderful woman and the perfect match for Pygmalion. She used to take us kids down to the bayou to hunt for snakes. And she loved to conduct tours around the museum. She'd get her friends to dress up like statues and then pop out at the visitors. Most of them loved it — no one besides Laverne Wright ever fainted, that I know of. Of course, that was long before I started animating some of the exhibits. But that was probably what gave me the idea.

"And best of all, Eugenie gave me some of the magic books I have now. She had gotten them from her father, Great-Grandpapa Bertram, after whom you are named. Well, a year or so after Grandma Eugenie died, Pygmalion said to my father, Pythagoras, one night at dinner, 'I'm still a young man.' He was eighty-six. 'Do you think it's too soon to start dating?' Pythagoras started to choke on his soup, and my mother had to slap him on the back to dislodge a noodle from his throat."

"You mean Pythagoras thought Pygmalion was too old for dating?" Bertram asked.

"He sure did. My father was a lot like your father," Poppa said. "In our family every other generation is weird and wonderful, like me. And the in-between generations are stuffy, like your father. I don't mean that your father isn't a good person, but he could — "

"Just enjoy himself more and not worry so much," Bertram finished.

"Exactly."

"If every other generation is weird, does that mean that I — "

"It doesn't bother you, does it?" said Poppa.

Bertram shrugged. "I'm not weird," he insisted. "I just happen to like some things that are a little strange, like magic and monsters."

"Well, what if people do think you're weird? Does it bother you?" asked Poppa.

Bertram thought for a few seconds. "I guess not, as long as I have you to be weird with," he said, giving his grandfather a hug.

Then he continued, "What did Pygmalion do when his son said he didn't want his father to go out on dates?"

"He went anyway. He said to me, 'Phineas, I'll be darned if I let that old idiot stop me from enjoying the last years of my life. You'll help me, won't you?'

"How could I say no?" Poppa continued. "When your father was born, and Pygmalion was already ninety-two years old, he met Jessie Mae. She was a spring chicken of seventy-nine. We had a big party to celebrate your father's birth, and even distant relatives were invited. Jessie Mae was a widowed great-aunt of your grandmother's.

"Well, it was love at first sight for Pygmalion and Jessie Mae. Jessie Mae lived up in Baton Rouge, and she arranged to stay for a few weeks with her sister down here. It wasn't three weeks later that Pygmalion announced he and Jessie Mae were getting married. Pythagoras made such a fuss about it that you'd think Pygmalion was going to leave her the business. One night Grandpa came to me and said, 'Phineas, I'm asking you for help one more time. I've decided to elope.'

"So, in the middle of one night, Pygmalion and I stole downstairs and went out to the driveway, where my car was parked. I had arranged everything with Jessie Mae's church up in Baton Rouge for their getting married the next day, and Jessie Mae was waiting for us at her sister's.

"Everything would have gone as planned, except we had had lots of rain, and I guess the car got a little damp. I was trying to start it up, but I had no success. Pygmalion, who was somewhat of a mechanical genius, went out to look under the hood.

"Suddenly, your great-grandfather, who was a light sleeper, flung the window open and confronted us. Just then, the car started. Pygmalion jumped in as Pythagoras came running down the muddy driveway in his nightshirt and cap. We took off like a race car at Daytona. In the rearview mirror I caught a glimpse of Father being splashed with mud from head to toe. Then I looked across at Pygmalion. He was grinning from ear to ear."

"Wow!" Bertram exclaimed. "That sounds like something we'd do to Dad!"

"Doesn't it, though?" Poppa agreed. "Pygmalion grinned the whole ride across town to pick up Jessie Mae. And he grinned the whole ride to Baton Rouge and the whole next day. I'd give anything to see that grin again."

Bertram sighed. Although Pygmalion had lived until the age of ninety-nine, he had died long before his great-great-grandson was born.

"I sure wish you could have known him,"

9

Poppa said finally.

"Well, why don't you bring Pygmalion back for a visit?" Bertram asked excitedly. "I can help, you know."

"*Visitation* is the more precise word," said Poppa with a wink. "And of course you can help. I had that in mind all along."

"Can we do it tonight?" Bertram asked.

"No, I don't think so," said Poppa. "It's already getting late, and if you're not back home soon, a certain Clark and Marie Potter will be down here to see what's keeping you."

At the mention of his parents, Bertram raised his eyebrows. They disapproved of the amount of time their son spent with Poppa in his lab. For people who ran a fun place like a wax museum, Bertram thought they were awfully dull. They didn't even believe in magic.

"When *can* we bring Pygmalion back?" asked Bertram, unable to contain his excitement.

"I have it on very good authority that this Saturday, the very same Clark and Marie Potter who live in this house will be in New Orleans for a small-business seminar!"

Bertram clasped his hands above his head in a victory pose. "I can't wait!" he cried.

"It says here in *The Babylonian Book of the Dead* that a few extra people at a seance isn't a bad idea," said Poppa.

10

"At a what?" asked Bertram.

"A seance. That's a gathering where people conjure up ghosts. Why don't you ask Adelaide and Wesley to join us?"

Bertram nodded. "Okay. You know what, Poppa? I think this is going to be our most exciting adventure yet!"

— Two —

In school the next morning Bertram waited for his best friend Wesley at his locker, but Wesley didn't show up. "Great," Bertram thought as he shuffled down the hall when the bell rang. "Now I'll have to wait until tomorrow."

But a few minutes later, Wesley slipped into class, trying to look invisible. That was kind of difficult, Bertram thought. Although Wesley was short — about three inches shorter than Bertram — he was at least twenty pounds heavier. That put Wesley in the roly-poly category. In addition, he had the habit of turning bright red in any and every embarrassing situation.

"Glad you could make it, Mr. Fairchild," Mr. Cranford said sternly.

Wesley nodded nervously and blushed as he took his seat next to Bertram.

"Meet me at lunch," Bertram whispered. "It's impor — " But just then the teacher called on him to read from their history book, so he didn't get a chance to tell Wesley what was going on.

That day at noon, Bertram and Wesley sat at their favorite lunch table, off to the side of the cafeteria. As he took a bite of macaroni and cheese, Bertram looked up and saw Adelaide Adelaide, the only girl in school with the same first and last name. When she neared their table, Bertram waved her over. "Sit with us!" he yelled.

"What did you do *that* for?" said Wesley, pushing his glasses up on his nose. Adelaide was not his favorite person in the world — and that was putting it mildly.

"Because I have something incredibly important to tell both of you," Bertram answered, "and I only want to say it once."

Adelaide brought her tray over and set it on the table. She had a streak of magenta running up the middle of her long, spiky blond hair. She and her parents had just moved to Black Bayou from Brooklyn, New York. Most of the kids looked at her as if she were an alien. But Bertram, with his love of the weird, had no trouble working up the courage to become her friend.

"Hi," she said.

"Have a seat," said Bertram.

"With *him* here?" said Adelaide. The feeling Wesley had for her was mutual.

"Only if you want to hear about the greatest,

13

most colossal thing that's ever happened at the Fear Factory."

"Better than the walking statue?" asked Adelaide.

"Much better!" said Bertram, barely able to keep his voice down.

"So what is it?" Wesley demanded.

"We're going to have a seance on Saturday afternoon. You know, we're going to conjure up a ghost. You want to come?"

Adelaide sat down immediately.

"Sure," said Wesley, pushing his glasses up on his nose again. "I've never met a ghost before." He paused a moment and looked thoughtful. "My uncle Fred had a friend who could talk to ghosts. Only he's been in this place called Twin Oaks for the last few years. The doctors won't let him out."

"Poppa says it won't work if someone doesn't believe in ghosts. So if you really feel that way, maybe — "

"I-I was just kidding," Wesley cut off Bertram. "I'm not saying I don't believe in ghosts. Although I'm not saying I do. I'd like to have a chance to see for myself, all the same."

"Well," said Bertram thoughtfully, "I guess you can come."

Bertram could see Adelaide getting that glassy look in her eyes she got whenever she was really excited about something. He was

14

puzzled when she didn't answer right away. Bertram couldn't imagine that she'd say no. The week before, she had admitted to having had her tea leaves read when she lived in New York. She'd had her palm read and her astrological chart done, too. Adelaide clearly didn't have a problem with the supernatural.

Finally she spoke. "I've never heard of a seance in the afternoon. Ghosts come out only at night."

"That's just in the movies," said Bertram, "so they can make it seem spookier. And remember — in Poppa's lab it can be as dark as night in the middle of the afternoon."

"Well, okay," said Adelaide. "I'll come. I don't have anything else to do Saturday afternoon anyway. But if it doesn't work, remember I told you why."

Adelaide was trying hard to sound uninterested, but Bertram could tell she was excited about the seance. "What ghosts are we going to invite?" she asked.

"My grandfather wants to conjure *his* grandfather Pygmalion," Bertram replied.

Adelaide looked disappointed. "I thought we might try for some dead movie stars or rock singers."

"Well," said Bertram, "after we're sure the spell works, maybe we can."

Adelaide seemed cheered by that idea, and

15

Bertram returned her smile. Nothing made him happier than stirring up a little trouble with his friends and his grandfather. And now, the plan was on its way!

Saturday morning, Bertram was so excited he could barely sit still at the breakfast table. Dora, the Potters' housekeeper, had the weekend off so Bertram's mother was cooking breakfast. Marie Potter was far more at home in the office than she was in the kitchen. She spent as little time as possible cooking and baking — and it showed.

Bertram's father was taking dishes out of the cupboard and setting them on the table. As Bertram looked at his father, he tried to imagine himself at the same age. Clark Potter's dark brown hair was receding up his forehead, and he wore thick, tortoise shell glasses because he was extremely nearsighted. Even on a weekend morning, he was dressed in his usual white shirt, tie, and dress trousers.

Bertram shook his head. No, he would never turn out like his father.

Bertram found his parents easier to deal with, amusing even, if he thought of them as the "Clark and Marie Show." Right now, for example, they were doing their version of a morning talk show.

"Did you confirm our reservations?" Clark

asked Marie.

"Yes. We've already discussed that," said Clark.

"I do hope we're not clear across the hotel from where everything is happening, like last time," Marie continued, brushing a strand of red hair off her forehead. She was busy attempting to fry sausages on the stove.

"I've been assured we're on the same side of the hotel as everyone else at the conference," said Clark.

Marie smiled. "I just can't wait for the software exhibit."

"And don't forget the office-supply videos. They're so much better than leafing through catalogs."

Marie pulled out a cutting board and started slicing a loaf of French bread. "I'm especially looking forward to the session on publicity," she said. "I just never feel like we're doing enough to publicize this place."

"Dear, are the sausages burning?" Clark asked, sniffing the air.

"No, I don't think so," Marie answered.

"Then what's that black stuff coming from the pan?"

"Oh, my gosh!" said Marie. "You're right."

"You should know better than to attempt two things in the kitchen at once," said Clark. He sounded concerned.

"You're right, dear," said Marie as she lifted the skillet from the burner. She took each sausage out of the skillet and drained it on a paper towel on the countertop.

After finishing with them, she began to crack eggs into a bowl.

"Won't the sausages get cold before the eggs are ready?" asked Clark.

"I suppose, but if we put them in the oven, they'll get all dried out. How *does* Dora do it?"

"I don't know," said Clark. "We probably should just have had cereal for breakfast. We're going to be eating big meals all weekend."

"Yes, but I didn't want my family to think I was neglecting them," Marie said, nodding over at Bertram and Poppa.

Next to Poppa sat Sigmund von Breymer, who was Poppa's assistant. He was a short man in his fifties, with thick black hair, large eyes and a slightly demented look. He had worked for Poppa for such a long time — twenty-five years — that he was considered one of the family. Although he had his own ground-floor apartment on the other side of the Fear Factory from Poppa's, he came upstairs for all his meals. Before Sigmund had come to the United States, he had lived in Transylvania. The von Breymers were Germans who had lived in Transylvania for centuries.

Sigmund was going to take part in the seance

18

that afternoon. As Bertram glanced at him, Siggy's heavy-lidded eyes betrayed no sign that anything out of the ordinary would be taking place later that day. Neither did Poppa's eyes show anything besides a growing impatience to dig into the plate of sausages. Bertram worried sometimes that his own face gave everything away. But his mother and father, absorbed in serving breakfast and chatting about their upcoming seminar, didn't suspect a thing.

"Breakfast!" Marie sang as she finally deposited the sausage and eggs on the table, along with bread, butter, and jam. For dessert, there was a special treat — sweet-potato turnovers that Dora had made, and that Mrs. Potter had only to defrost.

"Now, dears," she began, "I want you to promise you won't get into trouble while we're away. We'll be back tomorrow afternoon, and I'll leave the number where we'll be. I'd rest a lot easier if Dora were going to be here. She's a sensible woman. And besides, I wouldn't have to worry about what you were going to eat," Mrs. Potter said.

Bertram caught Poppa's glance and rolled his eyes.

"I don't know which one of you I should put in charge of the other two," observed Mr. Potter. "You're all like kids."

"But I *am* a kid," said Bertram mischievously.

19

"Oh, right," said his father. "Well, just don't do anything you wouldn't do while I was here."

Bertram groaned under his breath. Then he said, "Go ahead — we'll clean up."

"How thoughtful of you," said his mother.

Actually, Bertram was just anxious to have his parents on the road already. The sooner they left, the sooner he and Poppa could start the seance.

Clark and Marie went down the hall to their bedroom to finish packing and soon were ready to leave. Bertram watched from the window as the car pulled out of the driveway and disappeared up the street.

"I'll call Wesley and Adelaide and tell them the coast is clear," Bertram said to Poppa.

"I've already got the lab set up," Poppa replied. "We moved the gate-leg table in from my living room and opened it up. It makes a nice round table for five people. And we have five chairs, too."

"Yes, I help your Poppa," said Sigmund. "Ve haf good seance like in old country."

Bertram waited for his friends downstairs by the entrance to the Fear Factory. Saturday afternoon was usually the busiest time of the week, but in the last weeks before Christmas, attendance dropped off. People spent more of their time in the shopping mall. Bertram usually helped out on Saturday, but with less business, his parents said he could have the day off.

Maisie Cunningham, Lou Johnson and Sue Ann Petit ran the wax museum on Saturdays. Maisie was in charge of the gift shop, Lou took tickets and Sue Ann conducted tours when there were requests for them. "They're my guests," Bertram said to Lou as he ushered Wesley and Adelaide past the ticket booth.

"All the same, I have to charge them," Lou said. "That's your parents' orders. No free passes."

"But we're not even going to see the exhibits," Bertram replied, annoyed. "We're spending the afternoon with my grandfather."

"I don't care, Bertram. Your father — "

Bertram didn't stick around to hear any more of Lou's nonsense. He signaled his friends to walk through the gate.

As Bertram expertly led the way down the winding corridors adjacent to the museum rooms, he had a growing sense that he was about to be part of something important. He gave his usual knock on the door to Poppa's apartment.

"Greetings, my friends," said Poppa gallantly as he opened the door. The small group went back past the kitchen, through the living room and into the lab, where Sigmund was already seated at a table set for lunch.

"What's all the food for?" Wesley asked.

"We can't summon ghosts on an empty stomach, now can we?" said Poppa, smiling.

He had prepared one of Bertram's favorite meals — bologna sandwiches on white bread with mustard on one slice of bread and mayonnaise on the other. There was root beer to drink, and there were doughnuts for dessert.

"Dig in!" Poppa urged.

Bertram, Wesley and Sigmund needed no further encouragement. Wesley ate almost anything, and lots of it, which accounted for his shape.

Adelaide, however, just watched them, looking disappointedly at the lunch that Poppa had prepared.

"What's the matter, dear?" Poppa asked.

"I don't think I can eat any of that," Adelaide told him. "I've recently become a vegetarian."

"A what?" said Wesley between bites.

"Vegetarian, you know. I only eat vegetables and grains, and healthy things like that. No junk food," she said. "Oh, really? Then how come last Monday, I saw you eat a hot dog at lunch?" said Bertram.

"That was almost a week ago," said Adelaide. "Things change a lot in a week."

"Well, I'm sorry, but I don't have anything else to eat," said Poppa. "If Dora were here, it would be different. She usually has some rice and beans, at least."

Adelaide looked hungrily at the lunch table. "Well," she said, "maybe just this once. Those doughnuts do look awfully good. But let me wash my hands first."

"Vegetarian," Wesley repeated when Adelaide was out of the room. "She's full of bologna!" He laughed at his own joke.

Adelaide soon rejoined the group and bolted down two bologna sandwiches and three doughnuts, followed by a large glass of root beer.

Finally everybody was finished, and Poppa cleared the table. He lit two candles in the center of the table, then put out the lights.

"See what I mean about the lab being dark?" Bertram said triumphantly to Adelaide.

"Okay, so you were right," she answered. "Big deal." Adelaide hated to be wrong.

Poppa said, "Please, we can't have any bickering. Ghosts don't like to come to places where there's arguing. We all have to create a loving atmosphere for the spirit. That's what it says in Mr. Daniels's book. Now let's all join hands."

"Let's all *what?*" said Wesley, his voice squeaking.

"Join hands," Poppa repeated.

"No thanks," said Wesley, who was sitting between Adelaide and Sigmund.

"Yuck," Adelaide seconded.

"You two listen to what Poppa says or else you'll have to go home," said Bertram, who couldn't wait any longer to start.

"Holding hands is how we begin to call the spirit," said Poppa. "We have to make a chain of energy among all those present at the table."

Wesley looked disgusted, but he took Adelaide's hand. And she didn't pull it away from his. "Now we must concentrate," said Poppa in a soothing voice. "We close our eyes and clear our minds of all thoughts."

The room became so still that Bertram found it eerie. He felt as if time were standing still, as if the room they were sitting in had completely disappeared.

Then Poppa began to chant in a language Bertram had never heard before: *Nam runghi falto pane. Pane ixdar, pane mukdar. Falto, falto, mendi nadar.* Poppa paused, then repeated the chant. He continued in English, "If there are any spirits present, let yourselves be known. Is Pygmalion Potter present? We are looking for Pygmalion Potter. If any other spirits are present, please let Pygmalion Potter know that we are looking for him."

Nothing happened. Absolutely nothing. No one said a word, and Bertram started to feel the way he had before the chanting. Ghostly images started to float through his mind. His palms grew sweaty, although the rest of him felt colder. There was no doubt about it — a chill had entered the room. The hair on the back of

Bertram's neck began to stand on end.

Suddenly there was a loud tap-tap-tapping on the door to Poppa's lab.

Bertram jumped. "Who could that be?" he wondered out loud. "Oh, no, it's my parents!" he cried with alarm. "They must have decided not to go to their seminar after all!"

— Three —

"Come in!" Poppa called in a loud, cheerful voice.

The tap-tap-tapping stopped instantly, and the door to the lab creaked open.

Bertram and the others hesitated a moment, then turned their heads toward the door. Bertram's jaw dropped. Even Adelaide had nothing to say for once.

"Well," said a voice. "Why do you look so surprised? Weren't you expecting me?"

Instantly Bertram recognized the figure before him. Someone taking a quick look might have mistaken it for Poppa, but it was Great-great-grandfather Pygmalion, dressed in a fancy old suit. And he was carrying the same gold-handled walking cane he had in the picture in the hall.

It was Pygmalion, and yet it wasn't. Bertram could see the outline of his body, the outline of his clothes and even the features of his face.

But he could also see the doorway right *through* Pygmalion.

"You did it!" shouted Bertram. "I knew you could, Poppa. You're a genius."

Poppa was beside himself with joy. He seemed to have suddenly forgotten how to make his mouth work.

"After all these years, don't you have anything to say to me, Phineas?" the ghost said, addressing Poppa. "You called me, and high time it was, too."

"Grandpa! Pygmalion! It really *is* you!" Poppa exclaimed.

"Of course it is, Phineas. Now, why don't you introduce me to these people. Wait a minute," Pygmalion continued, floating toward Bertram. "This isn't Clark, is it?"

"No, Pygmalion. This is my *grand*son, Bertram. He's the one who will carry on the family tradition," Poppa informed his grandfather.

Pygmalion tapped his finger against his chin. "The tradition of eccentricity in every other generation, you mean?"

Bertram didn't want to be impolite to a ghost, especially in the first few minutes of his visit. But he felt he had to defend himself. "I'm *not* eccentric," he said, trying to be as polite as he could. "I just like magic and — and *ghosts* and things like that."

"We'll see," said Pygmalion mysteriously.

27

"Now, who are these other people, Phineas?"

Bertram spoke up instead. "These are my friends, Wesley Fairchild and Adelaide Adelaide — "

"I like your hair, Adelaide," Pygmalion said sincerely. "It's the latest style on the other side, too."

"And this is Poppa's assistant, Sigmund von Breymer," Bertram continued.

The small man smiled shyly and nodded.

"I never thought it would be like this," said Bertram. "I didn't know we'd get to talk with you just as if you were a real person. I thought maybe we would ask questions and you would knock out the answers on the table."

"That's child's play," said Pygmalion scornfully. "Your grandfather used quite a powerful spell to bring me back."

"*Rowl* !" said a voice from under the table.

"Oh, I forgot," said Bertram. "This is my cat, Fishbreath." The big orange tom stretched and crept cautiously out from under the table. The hair stood up on his back. He chased himself around in a circle three times, then jumped at Pygmalion. Or rather, jumped *through* Pygmalion. When the cat landed, he looked back at the ghost, then scurried off to hide in the living room.

"Friendly animal, isn't he?" said Pygmalion jokingly.

28

Wesley, Adelaide and Sigmund hadn't said anything since Pygmalion's appearance. Bertram guessed it had made them speechless. That fact did not go unnoticed by Pygmalion.

"Phineas and Bertram, your friends are all so quiet. I was always hoping that when I came back, it would be to something like a brass band," he said, frowning.

"If it's music you want, we could put on a record," said Poppa. "Or maybe you'd rather watch television."

"No, I see enough television where I came from. And you know, we don't need to plug it in. We just have big screens that pick up the images from waves that are broadcast on earth. What else is there to see?"

"How about the VCR?" Bertram suggested.

Pygmalion shrugged. "All right, whatever that is. We don't have that in the great beyond."

"Let's all move into the living room, and I'll show you," said Poppa.

"You won't disappear if we put the light on, will you?" Bertram asked.

"No, of course not," said Pygmalion. "You might not see me quite as well as in the dark, but I'll be around all the same."

The little group moved into the living room, and Poppa flicked on the light. After being in near-darkness for so long, Bertram had to squint a bit until they got used to the brightness. When he opened his eyes fully, Pygmalion was still there. The ghost was standing in front of the TV screen, which Bertram could see plainly through him.

Poppa quickly explained how the VCR worked. Pygmalion said, "We don't have your problem on the other side. When a show is broadcast, the waves just stay around forever. We can get any show we like. But I am interested in seeing some of those movies on tape. Now, what else do you have to show me?"

"Well," Poppa said, tapping his chin thoughtfully, "we could take a spin around the Fear Factory, but I think we ought to wait until it closes for the day,"

"Hogwash!" said Pygmalion.

"What will people say if they see a real ghost?" said Poppa.

"Phineas, I'm disappointed in you. Where's your sense of adventure?" Pygmalion asked. "Besides, if the tourists see me, they'll just think I'm part of the show."

"That *would* make a great special-effects exhibit," observed Bertram. "I suppose we could rig up a ghost scene easily enough."

"There's my boy, thinking again!" Poppa said, delighted. "I can see you're going to follow in my footsteps, all right." He turned to Pygmalion. "Where would you like to start the tour?"

"The Hall of Monsters, of course — my masterpiece," said Pygmalion.

"Uh-oh," thought Bertram.

Poppa led the way. He was followed by Pygmalion, then Bertram, Sigmund, Wesley and Adelaide. They headed for the far corner of the building, near the visitors' entrance. It was the original part of the museum, which was really a complex of old warehouse buildings joined together. It was the only section that Pygmalion had seen through to completion. Bertram looked around for any guests, but there was no one in sight. Pygmalion floated by the first exhibit, staring at it thoughtfully.

"I don't remember a vampire here," he said to Poppa.

"That's because there wasn't one in your day," Poppa replied.

"You mean you changed the exhibit?" Pygmalion said with annoyance. "What happened to my masterpiece, the werewolf?"

"Frankly, it was showing its age," Poppa said. "We change all the exhibits from time to time. After a couple of years, when lots of our visitors have seen the displays, we have to change things around so they'll want to come back."

"I don't believe my ears!" Pygmalion thundered. "I'm hardly cold in the grave and he changes the exhibits."

31

"It has been thirty-five years," said Poppa. "And a lot has changed since then. We have competition from theme parks and horror films, and even real life. It takes more to scare people these days."

"Hogwash!" said Pygmalion. "Great statues are great statues. You don't see them changing the display of the crown jewels In England just because everybody's seen them already."

"Maybe not," said Poppa confidently, "but in some art museums the paintings and other objects are moved around all the time."

"Well, maybe you have a point," said Pygmalion, "but I won't let you win until I've had a good look around."

"Then take a closer look at this vampire display," Poppa said, standing his ground. "Note the expression of horror on the victim's face."

Pygmalion looked doubtful. Bertram felt a little sorry for him. After all, he had only been back on earth for half an hour, and already he had discovered that his grandson had undone all of his work. But Bertram also knew Poppa had made the right decision when he had updated the exhibits.

"What about the layout, the overall concept?" asked Pygmalion suddenly.

"The layout, the concept?" echoed Poppa. "What are you talking about? You never had a concept. You made one statue, then another, then another."

"Maybe so, but I *did* have a grand plan," Pygmalion insisted.

"Yes, to fill up the room!" said Poppa.

Pygmalion ignored Poppa's last remark and floated over to the Bride of Frankenstein exhibit. "Look at this — tacky workmanship, phony-looking faces, not at all scary," he said, frowning.

"Pygmalion, this is the only display in the whole museum that's exactly as you made it!" Poppa cried. "Not a hair has been changed. I've kept it the same on purpose, as a tribute to this museum's founder — you!"

The ghost mumbled something to himself that nobody could hear, and then floated on to the re-creation of a scene from a horror movie featuring a human-sized fly. "What is this garbage?" he exclaimed. "And what on earth is that?" he asked, pointing to a scene across the hall that featured an enormous plant devouring a person.

"These are from movies that have come out since you — since you became a ghost," said Bertram, eager to be helpful. He was wondering if he would grow up to be as stubborn as his grandfather and his grandfather's grandfather. Stubbornness seemed to run in the family, just like weirdness.

"Who likes these things?" asked Pygmalion.

"Everyone," Bertram told him. "Visitors love to see scenes from their favorite horror movies. Look over here," he said, his voice rising with excitement. He couldn't control his enthusiasm. He loved what Poppa had done with this section.

There had been some horror scenes from old, classic movies, which were okay, but there was a lot more new, exciting stuff. The exhibits were changed on a rotating basis, and he and Poppa often went off to see new movies at the mall to get inspiration.

Pygmalion seemed to accept that he had been too quick to judge the new exhibits, so he began to back down. "I know I'm just being a crotchety old ghost," he said quietly. "But you should have prepared me for this. I had no idea that everything would be so different. No hard feelings, Phineas?"

"Of course not, Grandpa," said Poppa.

With that, Pygmalion gave his grandson a ghostly pat on the back.

"What's that I hear? Music?" asked Pygmalion.

"Yep," said Bertram proudly. "Poppa thought it would add to the mood."

Pygmalion rolled his eyes. "Well, the next thing you'll tell me is that you've put little motors on the statues to make them move around."

"Just wait," said Bertram.

The group was just about to enter the section of the museum known as the Rooms of Blood.

"Here we have a scene from the story 'Ali Baba and the Forty Thieves,' " Bertram continued. "This is the part where the trusty servant is pouring the hot oil into the casks."

"It isn't a bad exhibit, but how come there are only six casks?" Pygmalion said. "There were *forty* thieves."

"Because forty would have taken up half the space in the Rooms of Blood," said Bertram.

"Which leads me to another question," said Pygmalion. "Why is it in here? There isn't any blood involved."

"Because," said Poppa in an irritated tone, "we don't have a Room of Oil."

"Wait till you see the best part," said Bertram. As they drew nearer, all of a sudden the lid popped off the first cask. The servant woman grabbed a dipper, put it into a large bucket that was supposed to contain hot oil, and upended it into the open cask. Then the lid popped back onto the cask. This happened in turn with the other five casks.

"Amazing!" said Pygmalion. "I think I'm going to like it here. You'll see I'm not such a fuddy-duddy after all."

Bertram was happy. He began to think about Poppa and Pygmalion and himself. Pygmalion had started the wax museum, and he had made it pretty much what he had wanted to. He had based it mostly on what the people of his time were familiar with and what they wanted. Anyway, it had been a success. Then, after Pygmalion had died, Poppa had taken over running it. He had changed it according to his personal interests, and he had also paid attention to what other people wanted to see. As technology grew, he could mechanize almost whatever he wanted, and create special effects with holograms and fake steam and so forth.

When Bertram's father was old enough, he had decided that Poppa was no businessman and that he should run the business part of the museum. But even he was smart enough to realize that no one could beat Poppa's creativity. Bertram wondered what his contribution would be, and if Poppa's ghost would come back and find fault with *his* changes.

Now the group was standing in front of "The Pied Piper of Hamelin." It was based on the old poem, in which the piper rids the town of rats. The display was covered with rats — fake ones. Poppa had arranged the rats in lifelike swarms. They actually moved and, thanks to a cassette tape, appeared to make ratlike squeaks. It was the only display that Sigmund found disturbing — so much so that he had to cover his eyes whenever he passed it. Siggy absolutely hated rats.

Pygmalion got into the spirit and floated above the scene, pretending to be the Pied Piper.

Next they moved on to a scene from the French Revolution, showing a man who had just been guillotined. Aside from the bloody head, there wasn't anything particularly horrible. But the head was so lifelike that it made a frighteningly disgusting display all by itself.

Pygmalion bent over and examined the head. "All this space wasted for one bloody head. What could you have been thinking, Phineas?"

Bertram waited for Poppa's reply, but he only shook his head. He seemed to be used to his grandfather's constant criticism.

Finally they moved into the last, and most horrific, section of the Fear Factory — the Chambers of Doom. *I wonder what Pygmalion will say about this,* Bertram thought to himself. *This is a masterpiece of horror. People run out of here screaming, even though we warn them ahead of time.* The group entered the first chamber. It looked like one of those fun-house rooms where you can see yourself in mirrors an endless number of times.

"*This* is what you build, Phineas?" said the ghost. "A carnival attraction?"

"Just wait," said Poppa.

Gradually the lights began to dim, so that

the room was bathed in twilight — a strange, brooding twilight. Music, first almost inaudible, then growing louder and louder, issued from invisible speakers. The mood became spooky. Then all of a sudden a bat flew overhead. Through the magic of holograms and special projections, it seemed as if the bat would graze your head, no matter what height you were.

This was followed by bat after bat, coming from different directions, faster, faster, until the whole room seemed to be filled with bats. Their wings made swooshing noises, while their high-pitched voices drowned out the background music. A person, if slightly unbalanced, could easily become unhinged in the Room of Mirrors.

Eventually the bats began to disappear slowly. Their sweeps across the room and their noisy squeaking diminished. Finally all that was left in the room was the endless wall of mirrors.

A minute of silence passed until Pygmalion spoke up. "I'm truly impressed, Phineas. I still have my complaints about what you did to the Hall of Monsters. But you've redeemed yourself here."

"And you haven't even seen the rest of the rooms," said Poppa, quite pleased.

"They can wait. All this walking has made me feel like having something to eat."

"To eat?" everyone repeated.

"I didn't know ghosts could eat," said Bertram, astonished.

"Why not?" said Pygmalion. "It takes more than passing over to the other side to extinguish the famous Potter appetite!"

— Four —

Everyone crowded into the small eating area next to the tiny kitchen of Poppa's apartment. Sometimes, when Poppa was in the middle of working on something special, he and Sigmund would grab a quick meal there. He also used it to fix evening snacks for Bertram and himself.

"We still have some bologna left from lunch, if you'd like that," Poppa said to Pygmalion.

"Never liked bologna," said the ghost.

"What about doughnuts, then?" Poppa asked.

"That sounds good, to start with," said Pygmalion.

"If you're still hungry later — " Poppa began.

"Who said anything about hungry? Ghosts can eat if they want to, but they don't get hungry!" Pygmalion said with a smile.

"Why don't we all finish up the doughnuts?" suggested Bertram. He didn't want to see his share going to a ghost that didn't really even

41

need it.

"Good idea," said Poppa. He took out the sack and divided up the doughnuts. There were two for each person — and two for Pygmalion. "I'm glad I bought that extra dozen."

While Pygmalion ate, Bertram watched to see where the doughnuts went, but he couldn't tell. They just seemed to disappear once Pygmalion took a bite. Between bites, Pygmalion looked around contentedly, as if he were planning to settle back in at the Fear Factory.

"Now that I'm back," Pygmalion told Bertram, "I can't wait to pinch your father's cheeks, the way I used to when he was little."

"But, Grandfather, Clark used to hate that," said Poppa.

"Exactly," said Pygmalion. "That boy was impossible to have any fun with. And if he's grown up into a stodgy old man, then there's all the more reason to pinch his cheeks." Turning to Bertram, he said, "Sorry to talk about your father that way, but it's the truth."

"You're right," said Bertram. "Dad's really okay. But he can be *so* boring. The problem is, he doesn't have much of an imagination."

"Well, I hope he has enough of an imagination to keep the museum open, so you and all your folks after you have the supreme pleasure of living here," Pygmalion commented. Then he popped the last bit of doughnut into his mouth.

"He will, if Horace Q. Wright and his Citizens for Decency don't shut us down," said Bertram.

"Horace Q. Wright?" said Pygmalion. "Don't tell me — that must be Silas Wright's grandson!"

"The same," said Poppa. "And he's following in his granddaddy's footsteps. He has this screwball organization called the Citizens for Decency. Every few months they all dream up a new reason why we should close our doors. And the funny thing is, they expect us to listen to them."

"Oh," said Pygmalion thoughtfully. "Well, we can't let them close us down. But don't worry, I'll think of something."

"We don't spend too much time worrying," said Bertram. "Otherwise, there'd be no time to do anything else."

"Speaking of time," said Pygmalion abruptly, "what do you have planned for tonight, Phineas?"

"Tonight? I don't have anything planned. That is, nothing more than the usual — a cup of hot chocolate with Bertram," Poppa answered.

"That's awfully boring, Phineas," said Pygmalion. "How about a night on the town?"

"There's nothing to do at night in Black Bayou. You see, Pygmalion, there are some things that haven't changed in thirty-five years."

"When I said a night on the town, I didn't mean a night in Black Bayou. I was talking about New Orleans," Pygmalion said indignantly.

"We can't drive to New Orleans tonight," said Poppa. "I'm supposed to stay with Bertram until his parents get back tomorrow evening."

"Can't the boy stay by himself? He is eleven, after all. Or let Sigmund, here, stay with him," Pygmalion suggested.

"No, I gave them my word I'd be here," Poppa said solemnly.

Bertram wondered why Poppa didn't jump at the chance to go to New Orleans with a ghost. Then he remembered that his grandfather had had his driver's license revoked.

"Oh, all right. I'll confess," said Poppa. "I lost my driver's license."

"Then why don't you write away for a new one?" asked the ghost.

"No, that's not it. It was taken away from me."

"Why did you let that happen?" asked Pygmalion.

"I didn't have a choice," said Poppa. "The police did it. I can't understand it, though. I only took a shortcut through a park. I don't know why the police were in such an uproar. I stayed on all the paths."

"That's just like my Phineas," said Pygmalion, delighted by his grandson's creative answer. "Well, how about this for an idea? Why don't we all go to New Orleans?"

"Great idea!" said Bertram. "Only when will we get back? I'm not allowed to be out too late, and neither are my friends."

"You have a point," said Pygmalion. "Isn't there anything we can do around Black Bayou that's fun, Phineas?"

Poppa shrugged.

"Show me some of that old-time sparkle of the young man who helped me set up the 'tour and tea' for Silas T. Wright. Remember that, Phineas?"

"How could I forget?" said Poppa. "I was just telling Bertram about it the other day."

"It was the social success of the year," said Pygmalion. " *And* it kept the Wrights off our backs for a year."

"I beg your pardon, Grandfather," said Poppa. "But don't you remember what happened? Laverne Wright fainted dead away when Alain popped up in the middle of the Headless Horseman exhibit."

"Where do you get your ideas, Phineas? No such thing happened," said Pygmalion, hammering home his point with a rap of his cane on the table.

"What really kept the Wrights off our backs was what happened with the aquarium," Poppa said.

"What aquarium? Don't you mean the amusement park?" Pygmalion asked. "Bertram, you know about that, don't you?"

Bertram shrugged and shook his head.

"Phineas, doesn't this boy know anything?" said Pygmalion. "What kind of education have you been giving him?"

"The best kind," said Poppa. "Wax figures and magic, with some doughnuts and hot chocolate thrown in."

"Well, he doesn't know any *Potter* history," argued Pygmalion.

"Why don't you tell him *your* version of it?" said Poppa.

Pygmalion grinned. "All right, then. Well, it was the spring of thirty-seven — "

"Thirty-eight," Poppa corrected.

"No, Phineas. I'm sure it was thirty-seven . . . or thirty-six."

"Thirty-eight, but what difference does a year or two make?"

"Well, it was the spring of thirty-seven . . . or thirty-six . . . and Silas Wright was mayor, as usual. Silas had wangled some government money that was going around to help put people to work. And he decided he wanted to do something grand for the town at the same time,

46

something for which he'd be remembered. He decided to build an amusement park."

"Aquarium," Poppa corrected.

"No, I'm sure it was an amusement park," said Pygmalion insistently. "I remember he wanted to put his entire family to work in the sideshow." Pygmalion laughed a ghostly laugh and slapped his less-than-solid knee.

"Now, come on, Pygmalion. You know very well that it was an aquarium. The money had to be used for community educational purposes," argued Poppa.

"Well, that never stopped Silas Wright."

"Pygmalion, are you just pulling my leg, or what?" Poppa asked.

"Well, building the amuse — building the *whatever* meant lots of money for all of Silas's relatives and friends because they were all in the construction business. So he went ahead and had some plans drawn up. Well, Silas was so clever that while he was drawing up the plans for the amusement park, he figured out a way to get rid of the Fear Factory, too."

Poppa interrupted. "You know, the real reason the Wrights hated the Potters in those days wasn't because they objected to the Fear Factory. Silas wasn't a party poop like his grandson, Horace. No, it was because we made lots of money, without having to cheat and steal and threaten other people."

"Right you are, Phineas," agreed Pygmalion. "Anyway, to get back to Silas's plans. They called for a lagoon to be created up the bayou. Now, you know that I founded this wax museum on a mound of land that rises a little higher than the surrounding area. In order to make the lagoon, Silas planned to build a dam and divert the water into a new stream that would run through the lowland and cut us off from the rest of town. When I got wind of that, I made up a petition calling for a town meeting and I got people to sign it. Then — "

"Excuse me, Pygmalion, but you've got it wrong. *I* was the one who found out about the dam."

Pygmalion ignored Poppa's remark and continued. "Anyway, I took around the petition and got the town to back me. We had a rip-roaring town meeting, which was interrupted by six men dressed up as Indian warriors. They claimed that they really owned the land the Fear Factory was on, and trying to save it made no sense. Then one of them waved around a deed.

"Of course, Phineas and I didn't believe for a minute that the deed was real. I discovered that two of the 'Indians' were really cousins of Silas's from Port Arthur, Texas, and the others were their pals."

Poppa looked doubtful. "No," he said, "that

didn't come out until afterward. And by then, Silas had already given up. It turned out that the surveyor's report showed that by building the dam and the lagoon and the jetty, they were in danger of raising the water level by Silas Wright's waterside home. He could have wound up with a backyard full of water snakes!"

"Well, maybe you're right, Phineas. But I don't remember it that way at all. The digging company they hired, which belonged to Silas's wife's cousin, started making the lagoon in the wrong place. They dug up some poor guy's yard and flooded his house and they went bankrupt paying him for damages," Pygmalion finished the story.

"You know, I'm beginning to think we lived in two different towns," said Poppa, "and they just both happened to have mayors named Silas Wright."

"Well, what difference does it make, after all?" said Pygmalion. "We stopped him, and that's that."

"Now we just have to deal with his grandson, who seems to be worse," said Bertram.

Suddenly a grin spread across Pygmalion's ghostly face. "I know the perfect place to have some fun in Black Bayou," Pygmalion said. "Let's pay a call on Horace Q. Wright."

"What a great idea!" said Bertram.

"We just have to make sure of one thing,"

said Wesley. "We can't do anything that will make him madder at your family than he already is."

"You're right," said Bertram. "But since no one believed him when he said that Poppa made The Man Being Boiled Alive walk, who's going to believe that he saw a ghost?"

Poppa rubbed his hands together in excitement. "I'll bet our fine mayor hasn't been visited by a ghost before, not even after his worst bouts of overeating. I can't wait to see the look on his face when he realizes it's you — "

"Oh, it will be glorious!" said Pygmalion, kicking his heels together without making a sound.

"Tell me, Phineas, is Horace married? Does he have a family?"

"Married?" said Poppa. "He married a horrible woman named Nanny Dupin. They have two sons who are in their twenties. The boys have the worst qualities of Horace and Nanny put together. Neither of them has ever worked a day in his life. The older one got thrown out of at least seven schools that I know of."

"Well," said Pygmalion, "it sounds as though Horace and Nanny deserve sons like that."

"True," said Poppa, "but the rest of the town doesn't deserve having to put up with them."

"Well, that's convinced me that we shouldn't waste another minute. Let's go to

Horace's now."

"Hooray!" shouted Adelaide. She was still angry at the mayor for saying some nasty things to her when she was helping Bertram and Poppa track down the walking statue. She couldn't wait to get even.

"Perhaps we should wait till dark," suggested Poppa. "I think it will be much more effective."

"I'm all fired up to go now," said Pygmalion, "But I suppose you are right for once, Phineas. I do want to give this my finest effort."

"But what shall we do while we wait, Phineas?" Pygmalion continued, "Now that I'm back after all this time, I want to have some fun."

"Why don't we put on a little show," said Poppa, "like in the old days?"

"What kind of show?" Pygmalion asked.

"Why, juggling, of course!" said Poppa.

"Juggling?" said Pygmalion. "Great idea! You do you remember when we juggled our way around the world, don't you?"

"Do I!" Poppa said. "It was the year after I finished high school. Grandmother Eugenie had just passed on, and you were looking for something to help you forget. You were a mere lad of seventy-five — my age now. Wasn't that the time? I still can't figure out how we thought my father would run things while we were

51

away. Other than into the ground, that is — and he nearly did so. Luckily we arrived home just in time to put a little spark back in the old family business."

"Yes," said Pygmalion. "Although he didn't act exactly happy to see us. I could never figure out if that was just the case or if he was simply embarrassed for having made the museum so boring while we were gone. If I remember clearly," said Pygmalion, "it was the only year that a Wright *didn't* threaten to close us down." He and Poppa chuckled.

"Now," said Poppa, rummaging through the cupboards and the tiny refrigerator, "what do we have to juggle with?" He came up with two apples and an orange.

"Not those," said Pygmalion with disapproval. "I've never liked mixing apples and oranges."

"Well, it's that or nothing. I'm too out of practice to juggle glassware or dishes."

Pygmalion and Poppa entertained the rest of the group for a half hour with their juggling. As they got better, they got bolder, but Poppa still drew the line at glassware.

"I don't know, Phineas," said Pygmalion. "You just don't have the same spunk you used to have."

"I have plenty of spunk," Poppa snapped. "It's just that I don't have an expense account

53

for new glassware."

Bertram glanced at his watch and saw that it was close to five o'clock. "What do you say we clean up here and get ready to go to Horace's?"

"Time's a-wasting!" Pygmalion cried enthusiastically. "Let's get that guy — and good!"

— Five —

By the time the group filed outside, the Fear Factory had closed for the day. The last of the visitors' cars was pulling out of the parking lot.

As they approached Poppa's old convertible, Bertram overheard Poppa say, "But Pygmalion, I think it'd be better if you rode inside and hid on the floor."

"Absolutely not," said Pygmalion. "After all these years, I'm not going to stay cooped up inside your old ugly car when I can *float* along on top."

"What if someone sees you?" asked Poppa.

"What *if?*" echoed Pygmalion. "Who would believe their own eyes?"

"Good point," said Poppa. "But what if we lose you? Are you sure you can keep up with the car? Black Bayou has changed a lot in all this time."

"*Harrumph,*" Pygmalion said. "You're even more of a poop than I remembered."

"I am *not* a poop," Poppa protested. "Ask Bertram. Ask anyone."

"Well, then, prove it by letting me ride outside the car without a fuss. I'll hold on. Ghost's honor!"

"Oh, okay," said Poppa. "In that case, ride outside. But don't complain to me if something happens."

Sigmund slipped behind the wheel of the car, propped up on several seat cushions so he could see the road. As the rest of the group got in the car, Adelaide, who was sitting behind Sigmund, tried to smooth over the disagreement by engaging Pygmalion in conversation.

"Mr. Potter," she shouted, "what's it like to be a ghost?"

"Well, things certainly look a lot different from the last time I was here," Pygmalion commented from above.

Adelaide waited for him to continue. When he didn't, she asked, "Is it nicer?"

"Do you know the expression 'walking on air'? Well, that's kind of what it's like."

"Is it more fun?" Adelaide wanted to know.

"I don't know yet. Ask me when we get to Horace's house," said Pygmalion.

Wesley was sitting on the other side of the car, so he had to strain to be heard. "What's it like to be dead?" he yelled to Pygmalion. "Is it true that you're reunited with all your old relatives and friends after you die?"

"Oh, some spirits meet all their loved ones. But they have pretty careful rules up there. Take me, for instance. I've seen my whole family except for my first wife, Eugenie. I think for some reason somebody thought it best that we didn't meet, probably in case I mentioned Jessie Mae. They don't like fighting in the other world," explained Pygmalion matter-of-factly.

"Do you live in heaven?" asked Wesley.

"Well, that's a tough one," said Pygmalion. "I've never heard it called that since I've been there. But I'm sure it isn't the other place. And I don't think it's the one in between either."

"Well, what's it like?" asked Bertram.

Before he had a chance to answer, the car pulled to a stop at a red light and Pygmalion floated on ahead. He quickly turned and headed back to the car.

"What's that awful building over there?" Pygmalion asked, frowning.

"That? It's the new courthouse — the Silas Wright Memorial Courthouse," Poppa told him.

Pygmalion let out a cry of disbelief. "Where's the old courthouse?" he said, pointing to an empty parking lot next to the new building.

"Gone with the bulldozer one morning while half the town was still in bed," said Poppa. "So Horace's brother-in-law could build a new one."

"The scoundrel! Sigmund, step on it!"

Pygmalion ordered. "I can't wait to get to Horace's house."

Sigmund drove along through a section of town where the houses and gardens got bigger and bigger.

"Sigmund, you're going the wrong way!" said Pygmalion.

The driver paid no attention. He kept on going for a few minutes, then pulled the car to a stop at the corner of a small private street that ended in a wide curve. "What is this place? This isn't Silas Wright's house," said Pygmalion.

"No, it isn't," said Poppa. "Horace decided it wasn't grand enough for him. So he sold it, bought this land, and put up a brand-new house. It took so long to finish this that it wasn't ready by the time he had to move out of his old house. So he and the family stayed at the Black Bayou Hotel on taxpayers' money."

"Sounds just like his grandfather," said Pygmalion, shaking his head. "We'll have to see what we can do about him. Now, the rest of you hide in the bushes while I ring the doorbell. I know just the effect I'm after."

Bertram, Wesley and Adelaide could barely keep from giggling as they hid behind some huge azalea bushes near the front door. They were out of view, but they could peer around the large plants and see what was happening at the house. They also figured they could hear what

59

was happening, especially since Horace and Nanny had the habit of shouting even when they were only a few feet away from each other.

When Pygmalion rang the bell, Wesley whispered, "I'd like to know how he does things like that!"

"With energy, I think," Bertram whispered back.

"What if Horace and Nanny can't see the ghost?" asked Wesley.

"Why shouldn't they be able to?" Bertram wondered.

"I don't know," Wesley said with a shrug. "Maybe only people who believe in him can see him. I read that once."

"Well, it will still be a good trick," Adelaide chimed in as she squatted next to them. "Imagine how scared they'll be if the bell rings and they see *nobody* at the door!"

Pygmalion rang three times. Finally Bertram heard an upstairs window being raised. Nanny's voice, which sounded a little like a nail on a blackboard, said, "It's some old man, Horace. He's probably one of those people who are always collecting for some charity. They've been coming by ever since Thanksgiving. Why don't you go down and get rid of him?"

Then Bertram heard the window shut. Pygmalion left his spot on the front step and floated down to join the kids behind the bushes.

60

Finally the door opened, and there stood Horace in the doorway.

He yelled up into the house, "What old man? There's nobody here!"

The voice of Nanny screamed back, "What do you mean, 'there's nobody here'?"

"That's just what I mean," said Horace. "The old geezer must have left. If he saw you in the window, he might have been frightened away."

"Horace, you take that back," Nanny yelled.

"It's true. Are you forgetting you're wearing your beauty mask?" Horace said.

"You're right, dear," Nanny said.

With that, she closed the window, and Horace slammed shut the front door.

In a loud whisper Pygmalion said, "Now I'm going around to the back door."

Staying low to the ground, the three kids, followed by Pygmalion, headed for the back of the house. There they were joined by Poppa.

"What kept you?" asked Bertram. "And where's Sigmund?"

"I had to convince him to stay in the car, in case we need to make a quick getaway," said Poppa.

Bertram quickly filled Poppa in on what had happened. Poppa rubbed his hands together gleefully.

Then Pygmalion rang the back door bell.

Once, twice, three times. Finally Nanny's face appeared at an upstairs back window. Deep frown marks had cracked her beauty mask.

Flinging open the window, she shouted down, "Oh, it's you again! Go away! Whatever you're after, you won't get any here!"

Just then, Nanny caught herself, and she narrowed her already beady little eyes. "Wait a minute. Is that you, Phineas Potter? What are you doing in that getup?"

Before she could get an answer, she turned her back to the window and yelled into the house, "Horace, it's Phineas Potter, dressed up in an old-fashioned suit. Come see!"

By the time Horace reached the back window, Pygmalion had floated out of sight.

"Now, Nanny, dear, I think this beauty routine of yours has made you exhausted. You're seeing things. Why don't you go to bed? A good night's sleep will be the best thing."

"Sleep? It's only six o'clock!" said Nanny. "And I still have to take off this mask. Then I have to tone and moisturize."

"Well, whatever, dear. After that, you can go to sleep, then."

"You don't believe me, Horace Q. Wright! Have you ever known me to lie to you?"

"Well, no, dear, but there's always a first time. Maybe living with me has finally taught you something." Horace guffawed loudly.

With that, Nanny moved away from the window.

"Oh, no," whispered Bertram in the bushes. "I hope the show isn't over already."

"Not on your life," said Poppa. "I'm sure Pygmalion has only just begun."

Eager to see where Pygmalion had gotten to, Poppa led Bertram and his friends around to the front of the house. Pygmalion was hovering once more above the front doorstep.

He rang the bell and waited. From inside the front bedroom everyone heard the voice of Nanny shouting, "Now, what?"

By the time she came to the window, Pygmalion had hidden himself in the bushes with the rest of the group. "I like to build suspense," he said with a wink.

In her confusion, Nanny had forgotten to close the bedroom window. Everyone could hear her and Horace as their voices boomed above them.

"But you did hear the doorbell ring, did you not?" Nanny said.

"Yes, dearest," Horace answered.

"Then how could it just be strain and exhaustion?" Nanny replied. "The bell just doesn't ring by itself."

"I have no explanation, dearest. I just know that there's no one outside. I think it's all the strain that you're under, getting ready for our play."

"Play?" Bertram whispered to Poppa. Poppa shrugged.

"Maybe you're right," said Nanny. "After all, I've had to write the script, rehearse the cast, get the props. Come to think of it, there isn't anything I *haven't* had to do. I've almost had to play all the parts, too. Biff and Jerome may be my sons, but they certainly didn't inherit my dramatic talent."

"What about me, dearest? Don't I make a perfect Scrooge?"

"Oh!" said Bertram. "They must be rehearsing *A Christmas Carol*."

"I'll bet they're planning to perform it for their annual charity event," said Poppa. To Pygmalion, he explained, "Horace and Nanny have some kind of benefit every year just before Christmas. Last year they did a musical review, and the year before they put together a circus."

"Are they any good?" asked Pygmalion, wide-eyed.

"Put it this way," said Poppa. "Horace is a better mayor than an actor. Do you get the point?"

"Shhh!" whispered Adelaide. "I can't hear them."

But there was nothing more to hear, at least not at that moment.

Pygmalion broke the silence. "The thing that amazes me most is that the Wrights would do *anything* for charity."

Poppa said, "No one has ever been able to get close enough to find out *what* charity the money goes to. My guess is that it goes to the Citizens for Decency, as well as to Horace and Nanny's annual vacation fund. But no one who wants to do business with Horace dares to stay away."

"I see," said Pygmalion, gently tapping his cane on the ground. "Maybe this year *we* can cook up something special for the charity benefit."

"That would be great!" whispered Bertram.

"Now, to the matter at hand," said Pygmalion, and he began to float out from behind the bushes.

The little group watched as the dapper ghost reached a spot in midair just opposite Nanny's open bedroom window. He reached out and tapped with his cane on the brick beside it.

"Horace, it sounds like a shutter is banging," said Nanny. "Please go see what the matter is."

"I can't right now, dearest," said Horace. "I've just put shaving cream all over my face."

"I don't see why you can't go to the window with shaving cream on your face," Nanny declared. "I'll just have to do it myself, like everything else around here!"

With that, she flounced toward the window. Pygmalion floated right in front of the open sash. As Nanny came face to face with him, her eyes just about popped out of their sockets. Then she let loose with a blood-curdling scream.

— Six —

Bertram, Poppa, Adelaide and Wesley rolled about behind the bushes, laughing noiselessly until they felt as if their sides would split. Before Horace could reach Nanny at the open bedroom window, Pygmalion floated down to join the group in the bushes.

Poppa finally got himself under enough control to whisper, "Bravo!"

"You were great," Bertram gasped between giggles.

They could hear Horace at the window now. "But honestly, dearest, there's no one out there. Besides, how could anybody stand outside this window? It's fifteen feet off the ground."

"Then he *climbed* up. I tell you, Phineas Potter was outside my window, dressed up in old-fashioned clothes."

"What kind of clothes?"

"The kind of suit that gangsters wore in the movies fifty or sixty years ago. And he had a

67

gold-tipped cane," said Mrs. Wright.

"Now I know you've been under too much strain," said Horace. "You've just described Phineas's grandfather, Pygmalion. You remember my telling you about him, don't you? But he's been dead for years. Don't tell me you're seeing ghosts now!"

"Horace Wright, you know me better than that," Nanny said indignantly.

"Yes, dear," Horace said in a bored voice. "Now, why don't I just get you a nice hot cup of milk? And then you can lie down and try to get some sleep." With that, he closed the window.

After a safe amount of time, the little group crept out of the bushes and, keeping low, made their way to the car.

"Pygmalion, you were wonderful!" said Poppa.

"Just wait till you see my encore," said Pygmalion.

"You mentioned before that we'd cook up something for the play," said Bertram. "What kind of tricks do you have up your sleeve?"

"Well, I don't have any yet, but I'm sure it won't take me long to think of something. And you all can help."

Bertram quickly told Sigmund what had happened. Siggy was obviously unhappy that he had missed the entertaining scene, but he didn't complain. He just started up the car and drove them back toward the Fear Factory. Pygmalion rode along on top of the car once again. This time, Poppa didn't give him an argument.

"Oh, this feels wonderful!" said Pygmalion. "Although, Phineas, I think you should do something about the fumes from this gas guzzler."

"This is not a gas guzzler!" Poppa said with outrage. "It happens to be a vintage car. Besides, where did you learn that expression?"

"From television, of course," said Pygmalion.

Bertram changed the subject. "Sigmund, would you mind dropping off Wesley and Adelaide at their houses?"

"I vill do it gladly," said Sigmund.

First he dropped off Wesley.

"Call me tomorrow," Bertram said. "Maybe you can come over."

When they reached Adelaide's house and she got out, she called back, "This was fun! You can invite me to a seance anytime. Good-bye, Mr. Potter — both Mr. Potters."

"I'm not leaving so soon," said Pygmalion. "I imagine you'll see a lot more of me."

Bertram, Poppa, Siggy, and Pygmalion returned to the lab. While Poppa made hot chocolate, Sigmund plopped himself into a chair. Bertram picked at some doughnut crumbs, and Pygmalion perched on the counter.

69

"So, what's next?" Bertram asked.

"Well, I figure we have to come up with something really grand for the play," said Pygmalion.

"Haven't you done enough for now?" said Poppa. "I can't remember when I enjoyed myself so much, but why don't we just call it a night? We can do it again some other time."

"What do you mean, Phineas?" asked Pygmalion. "It isn't nearly time for me to go back yet. This is like a vacation. Everybody is entitled to a vacation once in thirty-five years. Besides, I haven't nearly finished with Horace Wright."

"Oh, please let him stay," said Bertram. "We can have lots of fun."

Poppa looked into Bertram's pleading eyes.

"Please," said Bertram.

While Poppa was deciding, Bertram wondered if his grandfather was a little jealous of Pygmalion because he was getting all the attention. He decided that it was up to him to remind Poppa that *he* was the one who had brought Pygmalion back in the first place.

Bertram took Poppa aside. He said, "I know you and Pygmalion are having a hard time getting along. But why don't you both just try? After all, don't you want to see more results of your genius?"

"My genius?" asked Poppa, totally puzzled.

"Yes, it was an act of genius that brought Pygmalion here in the first place," Bertram reminded him.

"I suppose it was," Poppa answered, puffing himself up. "I guess I am a genius."

"Of course you are," said Bertram.

"Oh, okay," said Poppa. "Pygmalion can stay."

"Yay!" shouted Bertram. Then he and Poppa rejoined the others.

"Well, I see that grandson of yours has talked some sense into you," said Pygmalion. "It's a good thing, too. I wouldn't want to miss Clark. When is he due home?"

"Not until tomorrow around noon," said Bertram. "They're leaving New Orleans for home after breakfast."

"I can't wait!" exclaimed Pygmalion.

"I suppose you'll have to," said Poppa.

The next morning Bertram slept late. By the time he got up and ate his breakfast, his parents were almost due to return home. He had just about enough time to slip down to Poppa's lab to check on Pygmalion.

"Blamed if I know where that ghost has gotten to," said Poppa. "I was worried something like this would happen. That's the trouble with ghosts. They're so independent!"

"Where do you think he might be?" asked Bertram.

Poppa shook his head. "That's the problem. He could be anywhere."

"Do you think he might have gone back to the other side?" Bertram asked.

"He can't do that. At least he's not supposed to be able to without my help, since I summoned him. Unless another ghost comes from the other side and he goes along willingly, I'm supposed to be the only one who can get rid of him. Although I must have his cooperation, too," Poppa explained.

"Well, good luck. I'll come help you look as soon as I can," Bertram promised. "I'd better get back to our apartment so I can be there when my parents come back. I don't want to make them suspicious."

Bertram darted through the maze of hallways that ran along the outside of the museum portion of the building. He had just reached his living room when he heard the sound of tires on the driveway. Looking out the window, he spotted his parents. "Whew!" he said. "Just in time."

He ran out to help them unload the car. "Thank you, Bertram," his mother said, "but I think we can handle the luggage. You know how lightweight the suitcases are because we never overpack. Tell me, did anything happen while we were gone?"

Bertram shifted uneasily from one foot to the

other. He didn't like to lie to anyone, especially his parents. So he always told them the truth. They never believed him, anyway. They always thought he was joking.

"Poppa conjured up the ghost of his grandfather Pygmalion," Bertram said in a matter-of-fact voice. "I invited my friends over, and we all had a good time." Bertram decided he could leave out the details, like going over to Horace Wright's house and scaring the wits out of his wife.

"That's nice, dear," said Bertram's mother. "You have the strangest imagination." Turning toward her husband, she added, "I'm sure it's from spending too much time with that father of yours. Don't you think so, Clark?"

Bertram's father grunted, which was his all-purpose response when he didn't really want to get involved in a conversation. Changing the subject, Mr. Potter said, "I think after we unpack, I'd like to take a nap."

"That sounds like a good idea," said Bertram's mother. "What time is Dora due back?"

"Around four," Bertram told them.

"Good. Then she can take care of supper tonight."

Bertram was glad Dora would be home soon; his mother was a terrible cook. He couldn't wait for dinner, either!

That evening at supper, as Bertram's father was passing the bowl of fried okra, he said, "You know, I had the strangest dream before, when I was napping. Bertram, you must have given me the suggestion when you were joking around right after we came home. Dad, do you remember how Great-grandfather Pygmalion used to pinch my cheeks all the time? Well, I dreamed he came here for a visit — right up here to my bedroom — and he was pinching my cheeks just like he did when I was a boy. And you know, when I woke up, it hurt as much as it used to. I realize people sometimes think they feel things in dreams, but cheek pinching is rather strange, don't you agree?" Clark Potter asked his father.

At that moment Bertram caught Poppa's eye, and almost choked on the biscuit he was eating.

Mr. Potter immediately began to pound Bertram on the back, and when his son continued to sputter, but less violently, he patted him on the back a few more times. When Bertram calmed down, Clark continued as if nothing had happened.

"What do you think of that?" he said to Poppa. "I only brought it up because I know how much you like weird things."

Even though he had recovered from choking, Bertram still felt more than a little uneasy. He and Poppa had searched all afternoon but hadn't had any success in finding Pygmalion. Who knew what kind of mischief a ghost might get into!

Suddenly the doorbell rang. The Potters had a separate entrance to their apartment above the museum, a door at the driveway side of the property.

"Now, who can that be?" Bertram's father asked. "Nobody comes calling on a Sunday evening."

"I might be able to do magic, but I can't see through walls and floors," said Poppa, trying to make a joke.

Dora poked her head into the dining room. "You all just sit where you are. I'll get the door. I'm already up."

A minute later, Bertram heard feet pounding up the stairs to the family apartment. Then, through the open archway from the hall, Horace Q. and Nanny Wright walked in, followed by an apologetic-looking Dora.

"I tried to stop them," she said, "but you might as well try to stop a bulldozer."

"That's all right, Dora," said Bertram's mother reassuringly.

"Potter!" thundered Horace Q. Wright.

Poppa took a long drink of water and said calmly, "Which Potter are you addressing? There are four of us here."

"I am addressing you, Phineas Potter. And you know why."

"I might do a little magic now and then," said Poppa coolly, "but I don't read minds. If you have something to say, say it. Don't keep us guessing. The rest of my dinner will get cold."

Out of the corner of his eye, Bertram saw Nanny hungrily eyeing the plate of biscuits.

"Phineas Potter, what do you mean by coming to our house last evening and scaring my wife out of her mind?" demanded Horace Wright.

"Dad, is that true?" asked Bertram's father.

"How am I supposed to have scared your wife, Horace?" Poppa asked, slyly winking at Bertram.

"Well — why don't you tell the story, dear," Horace suggested, nodding at Nanny.

She pointed her index finger accusingly at Poppa. "You know very well it was you outside my bedroom window. You were wearing that makeup that made you look older, and those funny old clothes, but I know it was definitely you. There's no mistake about it." Nanny began to flush.

"Nanette," said Bertram's mother, "you say my father-in-law was outside your bedroom window? Was he standing on a ladder?"

"Why, no!" said Nanny.

"Then maybe you can explain how he managed to support himself outside a second-floor window."

"Well — I don't know," said Nanny, becoming more and more flustered. "All I know was that he *was* there."

At that moment Bertram noticed Pygmalion, peering out around a corner, laughing silently.

"Dad, when did you learn to levitate?" Clark Potter said jokingly. Bertram knew that if anything brought out the sense of humor in his father, it was an attack by Horace and Nanny Wright.

"Right after I bought the old clothes and makeup that gives me a more, uh, *mature* look," Poppa said in a snooty tone.

"Now, you stop making fun of us," said Horace. "This is serious business."

"Just like that nonsense a while back about my father being able to make a statue walk?" asked Bertram's father. "Do you expect anyone to believe such silly rantings?"

"I'll give you 'silly rantings,'" Horace retorted. "When I succeed in having the Fear Factory closed down for good, you'll think differently about this discussion."

"I wasn't aware that this was a discussion," said Bertram's father. "When *I* want to have a discussion with somebody, I usually call ahead of time and make an appointment. Then I come in politely, not hurling accusations. Ridiculous ones, at that. Now, if you want to start all over again, I might forget the fact that you didn't make an appointment and that you disturbed our supper. What do you say to that?"

"I say, come along, Nanny!" Horace shouted, shaking himself as if a large ugly bug had landed on his back. "We don't want to be late for rehearsal."

As they lumbered back down the steps and out of earshot, Bertram's mother smiled gently. "You know, those two are getting weirder and weirder. They make this household look almost normal. Imagine Nanny thinking you could levitate outside her bedroom window, Poppa! And why you would want to, at that!"

"Thank you for your support, Marie," said Poppa, grinning. "And you, too, Clark."

"Don't mention it, Dad," said Bertram's father. "Although I must ask you something — did you conjure up Great-grandfather Pygmalion's ghost?"

"Who told you such a thing?"

"Bertram."

Poppa raised an eyebrow at his grandson.

"Of course, I know he's joking. Still, what a coincidence that Horace and Nanny should come around here squawking about you that way."

Bertram's mother giggled. "I'd give anything to be a fly on the wall at one of their rehearsals.

That show of theirs ought to be a real doozy. That circus was strange enough last year. But to see that bunch actually trying to put on a real play is another thing entirely. I hear that in this *Christmas Carol*, Horace is playing Scrooge. At least the casting is inspired."

Everybody started laughing at the image of Horace Q. Wright as Ebenezer Scrooge.

Later, after dinner, Bertram caught up with Poppa in the hallway. "I saw Pygmalion watching while Horace and Nanny were here," he whispered. "But he left before I could say anything to him."

"Well, don't worry about it," said Poppa. "That may just have been the bait we needed. I have a hunch that Pygmalion will come to call. Meet me in my apartment in about half an hour."

When Bertram got there, he asked, "What's up?"

"Pygmalion is in the lab right at this very moment, just as I'd suspected. And we have the perfect plan," said Poppa. "What would you say to a new production of *A Christmas Carol* — starring a real ghost, and one that Horace Q. Wright didn't bargain for!"

"Excellent!" agreed Bertram. "Let's get to work."

— Seven —

"Well, Bertram, my boy," Pygmalion said when Bertram entered the lab. "I had a simply wonderful day."

"Where were you?" asked Bertram, a trifle annoyed. "We spent all afternoon looking for you."

"I went for a walk along the bayou. The weather was nice, and I thought I'd take the opportunity. I didn't realize I needed your permission."

"I don't like to lose a guest," said Poppa. "Of course, you're free to go where you'd like, but next time, please just let me know."

"Oh, all right," said Pygmalion with annoyance. "Now, let's not spoil the mood. I'm still enjoying that little visit by Horace Q. Wright and his wife. I can't wait to begin *my* rehearsals for their play."

"Great!" shouted Bertram. "I can just see their expressions when a real ghost shows up."

"Yes," said Pygmalion. "The only problem is, as your grandfather pointed out, they've probably changed the story around to fit their family. That's why I'm going to pay a visit to the Wrights while they're rehearsing, and see what I can see. If I'm lucky, I'll even get a copy of the script."

As Bertram and Poppa watched, Pygmalion floated through the wall of the lab. With a wave of his arm, he disappeared from sight.

"I can't wait until Pygmalion comes back," said Bertram.

"We may have a long wait," said Poppa. "I suspect the Wrights and their cast have a lot of rehearsing to do."

Bertram and Poppa passed the hours by playing chess.

Finally, Poppa looked at his watch. "You'd better get yourself up to your room," he said to Bertram. "The worst thing would be if you got yourself grounded because you didn't keep to your bedtime on a school night."

"Oh, all right," Bertram said with a loud sigh. "But you have to promise not to plan the good stuff until I'm there. Promise me you'll wait until tomorrow night."

Bertram needn't have worried. He found out from Poppa the next morning that there hadn't been a rehearsal at all the night before. It had just been Horace's excuse to get Nanny out of the Potters' house.

All that day Bertram thought about little else except Pygmalion and the play. "You look far away," said Wesley, who usually wasn't too observant, while he and Bertram were eating lunch. Bertram told Wesley all about the play and about Pygmalion trying to get a peek at the rehearsal.

"How about if I come over after school?" suggested Wesley. "That way, you might finish your homework and we could spend some time on this play thing."

"Great idea," said Bertram. "I'll tell Dora you're staying for supper, so she'll make three more portions of everything."

"Funny, really funny," said Wesley.

"And I'm sure my father won't mind driving you home tonight," Bertram went on. "Better that than have you stay all night."

"Okay, you're on," said Wesley.

Bertram and Wesley's homework took longer than they had thought it would. By the time they were done, Dora was calling them for supper.

Bertram and Wesley were too excited to say much during the meal, although the excitement didn't stop Wesley from eating the huge amounts of food he usually did.

After supper, Bertram and Wesley suffered in silence while they were helping clean up. They didn't want to seem too anxious to get finished with dinner in case Bertram's parents might suspect something.

Once they were finished clearing the table, they disappeared quickly down the corridors leading to Poppa's lab. "Won't your parents wonder where you are?" asked Wesley.

"No," said Bertram. "They know I'm with Poppa, and that's kind of all right, unless I get to bed too late."

When they reached Poppa's apartment, Bertram knocked on the door with his usual code, and Poppa was waiting for him.

Two hours passed, and when Pygmalion still hadn't returned, Wesley said that he'd better be getting home. He and Bertram sadly trudged back to Bertram's apartment, where Bertram's parents were watching TV.

Bertram's dad drove Wesley home, and Bertram went along for the ride. When they got back to the Fear Factory, Clark Potter said, "It's time you should be getting along to bed, too, Bertram."

"Aw, Dad," Bertram began, but his father put a quick end to his protest. Bertram wasn't the least bit sleepy. He was wide awake with expectation over Pygmalion's return from the rehearsal. Soon he heard his parents go off to their room, and all was still in the apartment. He knew Poppa would be up late as usual.

Without changing from his pajamas, he took a flashlight and left his room, closing the door after him. He made his way through the dark halls along the edge of the Fear Factory.

"What took you so long?" said Poppa jokingly. He knew it was hard for Bertram to sneak downstairs until his parents were in bed. "I've practically been splitting my sides waiting to work on our treat for Horace. Wait till you see the script Pygmalion brought back, and all the things he has to say about the play."

Pygmalion, for his part, was sort of sitting on one of the stools in the lab, looking quite pleased with himself.

"Just look at this," Poppa said to Bertram. "Nanny has rewritten the story. You know how the original one goes, don't you?"

Bertram shrugged. "I kind of remember it, but why don't you refresh my memory."

"Well," Poppa began, "there's this guy Scrooge, and he runs an office. He has no interest or patience in the merrymaking that surrounds Christmas. He's — well, he's a scrooge.

"Anyway, Scrooge has this employee, Bob Cratchit, whom he pays miserably. And Cratchit has all these children, including one called Tiny Tim. The Cratchits are poor, and Tiny Tim is sick, and poor Bob doesn't have money for the things they need.

"Scrooge rejects his own nephew's Christmas

party invitation, and he goes to bed. He is visited by the Ghost of Christmas Past, the Ghost of Christmas Present, and the Ghost of Christmas Future. They show him how he used to be a nice person, how he is mistreating people today, and then horrible images of what his future will be like if he keeps on the way he's going now.

"When Scrooge wakes up in the morning, he's a changed man. He welcomes his nephew and he brings all kinds of good things to the Cratchits, who are very grateful."

"Yeah, that's pretty much how I remember the story," said Bertram. "So how did Nanny Wright change it?

Pygmalion pointed to the script. "Instead of Bob Cratchit, Scrooge's loyal and poor assistant, there is now one Roberta Cratchit, to be played by Nanny. The young Cratchit children are being replaced by Biff and Jerome Wright. The rest of the play seems pretty much true to the original story."

Bertram noticed that the roles of the various ghosts were being played by people whose names he recognized as members of the Citizens for Decency.

"So are you going to be the fourth ghost?" asked Bertram. "That should pretty well break up the play. Nobody onstage will know what to do."

"I'd like to go for something more subtle,"

said Pygmalion. "How about if I pay a visit backstage to the Ghost of Christmas Future just a little before he's supposed to go on? That should put him out of the picture. Then I will go on in his place. The audience won't catch on right away, because I'll memorize the part and play it as the actor would have. But sooner or later Horace will know the difference. If they don't lower the curtain right away, I can have some fun with him."

"Brilliant!" exclaimed Poppa.

Bertram laughed mischievously and rubbed his hands together. "I can hardly wait till the curtain rises next week."

The Wrights had arranged to use the high school auditorium for their play. Bertram sat in a seat near the front and looked up from the program as Wesley and Adelaide entered the room with their mothers. Wesley's mother was short, round and pink skinned like her son. Adelaide's mother was a tall blond woman who would have been beautiful except that she always had a sour expression on her face. Bertram wondered if her expression had anything to do with having a weird daughter like Adelaide.

Bertram waved, and the four of them joined him, his parents, Poppa and Sigmund, who had saved seats. Bertram, Wesley, Adelaide, Poppa and Sigmund were too excited to talk much, but Wesley's and Adelaide's mothers chatted with Bertram's parents.

"Won't this play *ever* start?" Bertram whispered to Poppa.

"Just be patient, my boy," Poppa said.

Finally the lights finally began to dim, and the curtain rose.

Bertram could hardly believe his eyes. There was Horace dressed as Ebenezer Scrooge, barking out orders to the widow Roberta Cratchit. He could hardly recognize Nanny. He didn't know what had made her decide to look so pitiful. She was usually so vain about her appearance. But here she was in an old shapeless dress with a scarf tied around her head.

"Mr. Scrooge," she said in a feeble, crackling voice, "why don't you come to our house for Christmas dinner?" Without a pause, she went on to answer her own question. "Because we ain't got nothing to give you. We got no turkey," she said, "and no toys. It won't hardly seem like Christmas, that's why. I need a raise. My boys need new clothes. We need food."

"Never!" shouted Horace. "As long as I see to it, you won't get a raise as long as you live. I pay you too much already!"

"When's Pygmalion going to come on?" Bertram whispered to Poppa.

"Just be patient. The first and second ghosts

have to appear first," Poppa told him.

"Those aren't them, are they?" Wesley whispered as the two Wright boys, Biff and Jerome, came onstage.

"No. Those are supposed to be the Cratchit children."

Scrooge said to them, "Why don't you go out and help your mother instead of loafing?"

Biff said, "My brother, Tiny Tim, is sick. He is too sick to work. And I must stay home and look after him."

"He looks all right to me!" said Scrooge. "What's the matter with him?"

"He has the con — confusion!" Biff said.

The audience roared with laughter.

"I think he meant *consumption*," Poppa said to Bertram. "Nanny shouldn't have tried to doctor up the story."

"Yes, whatever happened to Scrooge's nephew?" Bertram asked.

"I'll tell you what happened," said the man sitting behind him. "I was supposed to be the nephew. But they cut the part because the Wrights didn't want to take any attention away from themselves!"

In the next scene Horace was in a nightshirt and night cap, getting ready for bed. Before he climbed into bed, he pulled a large box out from under the bed. It was supposed to contain money, which he was counting.

"I think they're mixing this character up with another one," said Marie Potter. "I don't remember a money-counting scene."

Before long, Scrooge finished counting, pushed the heavy box back under the bed, and got under the bed covers. As he fell asleep, the room darkened. But there was still plenty of light to see by.

"Horace looks like he really fell asleep," Clark said. But then Scrooge sat up in bed. He said in a forced, hammy voice, "What do I see before my eyes?"

"What indeed?" said Poppa, for there was no one onstage besides Horace.

The Ghost of Christmas Past had missed his cue. But he finally came into view, tangled in a length of rope. It was clear that he was supposed to have been flown in from above, but that the rigging hadn't worked.

The audience howled with laughter again.

"I am the Ghost of Christmas Past," said the actor when the laughter died down.

"Why, you're Marley, my old partner," Scrooge said. "What are you doing here?"

"I've come to show you what I've learned since I've passed over to the other side."

Poppa and Bertram exchanged knowing winks.

The ghost Marley was dressed in a sheet, with a hole cut out for his head. He managed to untangle the end of the sheet from the trailing rope. Then he approached the bed and reached out for Scrooge. Horace shrank back in the bed, but finally agreed to go along.

As he got out of bed, his foot got caught in the hem of his nightshirt, and he fell flat on his face. His night cap went flying across the stage. As the audience once more broke out into laughter, Marley helped him up. Horace's face was as red as a Christmas stocking.

"This is better than watching cartoons," Wesley whispered.

In the next scene, the Ghost of Christmas Present led Scrooge to the Cratchit home for what was supposed to be a peek at their bleak Christmas day. Nanny, Biff, and Jerome were behind a thin cloth, which was lit so that only their shadows were visible on an otherwise dark stage.

"Nice effect," whispered Poppa. "I think we could do something like that in the Fear Factory."

"Don't tell Horace you got the idea from him," Bertram whispered back. "When's Pygmalion going to come on, anyway? This is getting boring."

"Patience, my boy," said Poppa. "He's next."

Finally the stage went dark, and Scrooge reappeared in bed with just a dim light on him and the nearby wall and ceiling. Horace said in his most theatrical voice, " *Now* what do I see before my eyes?"

With that, Pygmalion floated in from the wings and hovered above Horace. He was dressed in a black shroud so that his face was only slightly visible. And he was holding a staff.

There was a spontaneous round of applause from the audience. The people thought they were witnessing a planned special effect — the first thing that had actually gone off without a hitch!

Bertram heard a woman behind him say, "Well, the rest of the play has been stinky, but it was worth it for this."

Even in the semidarkness, Bertram could tell that Horace's expression had changed from fake horror to real horror. The audience thought it was seeing a ghost whose supporting ropes were cleverly hidden — a magnificent stage trick.

But Horace *knew* he was seeing a figure with no supporting ropes. "Y-you're no stage g-ghost," said Horace in a low voice. "You're real!"

"Yes, I am," said Pygmalion in a creepy voice.

Horace's face went absolutely white. "Get me out of here!" he screamed, then jumped out of the bed and ran offstage.

A minute passed, and the audience began to

get restless.

"What's going on?" said a man behind Bertram. "Just when this play finally starts getting good, Scrooge runs away. Are they going to finish this or not?"

"Yes!" shouted a woman. "If not, I want my money back!"

Pygmalion, meanwhile, was enjoying the spotlight.

"You know," said Bertram's father to his mother, "from what I can see of that ghost, there's something familiar about him.

"It must be your imagination," said Mrs. Potter.

"I don't know," Bertram's father replied. "Poppa always says I don't have any imagination."

Suddenly screams of "Curtain! Curtain!" came from backstage. But whoever had been operating the curtain must have fled or gone into shock, for it didn't fall. Then Nanny Wright appeared, still in her Roberta Cratchit costume. She obviously intended to take matters into her own hands. From her seat backstage, she hadn't been able to see Pygmalion floating up. But as she charged center stage, she came face to face with him.

She pointed an accusing finger at him, but words failed her. Instead, she let out a wild scream, as she had at her bedroom window.

"*Eeeeeee!*" she cried.

She stood rooted to the stage, screaming, for nearly a minute. Pygmalion, unwilling to listen to her, floated off the stage. The audience didn't know what to make of the spectacle. They couldn't understand why both Horace and Nanny had been so terrified. Suddenly the screaming stopped, and Nanny seemed to be getting hold of herself.

In the silence that followed, a little girl said, "Maybe it *was* a real ghost."

"Don't be silly," said her older brother. "There's no such thing as a *real* ghost."

With a trembling finger, Nanny walked to the front of the stage. She pointed at Poppa and shrieked, "I don't know how you Potters did this, but I'll get you for it!"

— Eight —

Used to such insane outbursts by the Wrights, Marie Potter merely turned to her husband and said coolly, "Whatever does Nanny mean?"

Bertram's father shrugged. "Beats me."

Immediately afterward, Horace came down from the stage and walked along the front of the audience. Shaking a finger at Poppa, he said, "I don't know how you did what you did at my house, and I don't know how you did what you did here, but you did it! And I'm hopping mad. This time you've pushed me too far. I'll fix your whole miserable family, I will!"

"Really, Horace," said Poppa, shaking his head. "First you say I levitated outside your bedroom window. And now you accuse me of — what are you accusing me of, anyway?"

"You know very well. You spoiled my show. You came up on stage and made yourself into a real, live ghost."

"You flatter me, Horace, but what, may I ask,

is a real, live ghost? Everybody knows there isn't such a thing as a ghost," Poppa said matter-of-factly. "And besides — you can ask anybody around me — I was sitting in this seat the whole time during this play. Although I'm not sure why! It was a dreadful piece of claptrap!"

For once Horace was speechless.

Clark Potter rose from his seat and said to the rest of his family, "I think it's time to leave." He was followed out the door by his wife, Bertram, Poppa and finally Sigmund. Before they had left the auditorium, a voice rang out.

"Way to go, Mr. Potter!" Wesley yelled over the protests of his mother, who tried to clap her hand over his mouth.

"Yeah!" screamed Adelaide. She had been waiting for a long time to get even with Horace for the mean things he had once said about her hair. "This show is the worst thing I've ever seen!"

Other people in the audience took up the fight.

"The girl's right, Horace," said a man nearby. "You're acting like you've flipped your stack of flapjacks."

"You're not kidding," said a woman on the other side of the room. "Whatever happened with that ghost thing was wonderful, and I don't care where it came from. It was better than the rest of your stinking show. Why did you have to stop just when it was getting good?"

"You've got the right idea," said a man in the row behind her. "And what do you do when a show stinks? You leave!" With that, he got up. Other people, first in small groups and then in larger ones, also rose from their seats and poured out into the aisles.

"I think this is our exit cue," said Poppa, and the Potters left the room before the rest of the crowd could catch up to them. The last thing they heard was someone — probably a member of the Citizens for Decency — yelling, "Stop! Please come back! The show will go on!"

After they were safely through the door, into their car, and out of the parking lot, Bertram's father turned to Poppa. "Don't ask me to explain what happened on stage tonight, but all I know is that you had nothing to do with it. You couldn't have. You were sitting next to me the whole time. But now I remember who that ghost thing looked like — Great-grandfather Pygmalion. If there is such a thing as a ghost, do you suppose after all this time, Pygmalion has decided to come back for a visit?"

"Really, Clark," Poppa said. "And you accuse *me* of strange notions. We all know there isn't such a thing as a ghost, now, don't we?"

"Well, I guess so," said Betram's father, shrugging.

Halfway home, Bertram suddenly got the feeling he had left something behind. He felt in his pockets, but his lucky coin was still there, as was his handkerchief. Suddenly it hit him. They had left *Pygmalion* behind.

Bertram rolled down his window and stuck his head out to see if Pygmalion was riding on top of their car. But he wasn't.

"Would you mind closing your window, dear?" Bertram's mother asked. "It's getting chilly in here."

Bertram rolled the window up, and then caught Poppa's eye.

"Don't worry," Poppa whispered. "He found his way here. He can find his way home."

When they got back to the Fear Factory, Bertram asked his mother, "Can I stay with Poppa for a while? It's still early."

"Okay," said his mother. "But only till ten."

As Bertram and Sigmund walked Poppa back to his apartment, Bertram said, "I didn't think I could stand waiting for Pygmalion by myself. I hope he comes back before I have to leave."

They had just sat down inside Poppa's apartment when there was a tapping at the door.

"Pygmalion!" shouted Bertram, Poppa, and Siggy all at the same time.

"Of course it's Pygmalion," said the ghost, not waiting for them to open the door but just floating through it instead.

"We were afraid you might not find your way back," said Poppa.

"We're sorry we didn't think of you when all that ruckus started at the show," said Bertram. "We just kind of forgot."

"That's all right," said Pygmalion. "I'm used to getting around myself now, and I quite like it. I hitched a ride with your friend Adelaide and her mother."

"That's very resourceful," said Poppa. "Now, you've got to help *us* out."

"Me? How?" said Pygmalion.

"Well, so far, you've had a rather strong effect on Horace and Nanny. But instead of getting them off our backs, I'm afraid they're going to attack us even more fiercely."

"Really? Even after we made them sound so ridiculous with their accusations at the play?" asked Pygmalion. He seemed puzzled. "You heard what the audience thought of them."

"Yes, but you don't know the Citizens for Decency. They'll back up Horace on anything, even if it seems like a kamikaze mission." Poppa made the motion of an airplane crashing.

"Well, what do you do, just sit and wait for the attack?"

"What do you suggest?" said Poppa.

"Give me time. I'll think of something," said Pygmalion. "By the way, it won't be long till New Year's. What's everybody doing? You know, next to Halloween, it was always my favorite holiday. Never cared much for all that heavy food at Christmas."

"Well, we don't have any plans for New Year's," said Bertram.

"None of you? What a bunch of poops!"

"Well, I'll probably get to stay up till midnight, like last year," said Bertram.

"Who are you calling poops?" said Poppa. "We can have a good time. it's just that we haven't planned anything yet."

"Mom and Dad are having their usual New Year's Eve party," Bertram told Pygmalion.

"Yes," added Poppa. "They're having a bunch of their stodgy friends over.

"Perfect!" shouted Pygmalion. "I'll show Clark and his friends how to have a good time."

"Oh, great!" said Bertram.

"Then it's a deal," said Pygmalion. "Let's shake on it." He extended a spectral hand for Bertram to grab. It was like shaking hands with the air.

"Just don't do anything that will get us into trouble with their friends," said Poppa. "Clark and Marie need all the friends they can get in this town."

"No problem," said Pygmalion, "I'll be careful." Then he shook hands with Poppa as well.

"I only wish we could figure out some way for us to see the fun he's going to have at my parents' party," said Bertram.

"Well, why don't we? How about closed-circuit TV?" said Poppa. "We'll rig up a system so that we can watch what's happening at the party right on our own TV screen. Yes, that's brilliant! Sigmund can make something like that. I'm sure of it!"

"The only thing is, can we capture a ghost on TV?" asked Bertram. He was a bit skeptical about the whole plan.

"I don't see why not — I used to get ghosts on my old TV screen all the time." Poppa laughed at his own joke. "If worse comes to worst, we'll at least know when Pygmalion's around from the party guests' reactions."

"Oh, this is terrific!" said Bertram. "Now, how will we set it up?"

"Gif me time, I set up," said Sigmund.

The next morning at breakfast, Bertram's parents were discussing the previous night's events. "You know, Marie, maybe we ought to try a different tactic with Horace and Nanny," Bertram's father said. "We always wait until they attack us, and then we're on the defensive. How about if we extend our hand, say, in the Christmas spirit, and invite them to our New Year's party?"

Bertram couldn't believe his ears. *The Wrights sure are going to have a bad holiday season*, he thought to himself, stifling a giggle.

"You may have hit on something," said Marie. "In any event, I don't see what harm it would do."

Bertram didn't dare look at Poppa or Sigmund for fear of laughing and giving their plan away. But although he couldn't wait for Pygmalion to play tricks on the Wrights, he was also worried about the possible outcome of the evening. Later that morning, he confided in Poppa. "What if Pygmalion's showing up at the party just makes things worse between us and the Wrights?" Bertram asked.

Pygmalion, who was just floating by in the hallway, stopped for a second. "I heard that, Bertram, and I'm a little sad to hear you talk that way," he said. "For an unimaginative guy, your father has finally come up with a creative solution to a problem. I want to see that everything is forgiven, so I'm going to help the plan work. After all, I want to make sure my descendants live in this wonderful museum for a long time to come. Where else on earth would I rather visit?"

"Okay, I trust you," said Bertram. But he crossed his fingers behind his back for good luck, anyway.

For Bertram, Poppa and Sigmund, Christmas was almost overshadowed by plans for New

Year's. Their plan to watch the party on TV got an unexpected boost from a brand-new color set that Bertram's parents gave Poppa for Christmas. "He really deserves it," said Bertram's father. "His new exhibits helped make this the best year ever for the museum."

Sigmund got a new set, too, which made him even more eager to do his best hooking up the closed circuit.

"Fery simple," said Sigmund to Poppa, Pygmalion and Bertram, who were all assembled in the workroom where the statues were usually made. They knew they were safe there, because neither Mr. nor Mrs. Potter ever set foot in that part of the Fear Factory.

Sigmund continued, "Here I haf zis cable. I put one end into ze auxiliary hookup to ze new TV. Ze utter end I put into ze camera, vich I make from shpare parts."

"Spare parts of what?" Pygmalion asked, clearly fascinated. The latest technology was beyond him.

"Oh, a little of zis und a little of zat," said Sigmund. "I take book out of library, *How to Make Own Teefee Camera.* Fery simple. One qvestion only," he went on. "Ve can shtring cable like I show, or ve can haf remote. A little harder, but I can do. Vich do you vant?"

Poppa said, "Which do you think we can hide better?"

103

"Depends," said Sigmund. "Ze remote, I haf to fool around vit ze electricity. For ze cable, no. But cable shows. If Mr. or Mrs. Potter valk down ze hall, zey might see cable."

"How likely is that?" said Poppa. "Would either of them remember that the cable wasn't there the week before?"

"I guess not," said Sigmund.

"In that case, let's go with the cable."

"Goot," said Sigmund. "I fix so ve can control camera from your liffing room, yes?"

"That's a nice touch," said Poppa.

"Oh, this is terrific!" said Bertram.

"One more problem," said Sigmund, when the rest of the system was ready. "Vere do ve put up de camera?"

"Very simple," said Poppa. "Ahhh — "

"How about if we hide it in one of the beams?" Bertram suggested. The living room had fake wood beams that ran across the ceiling.

"Perfect!" shouted Poppa. "Sigmund is so good at that kind of work. He can cut a piece out of the beam, slip in the camera, then replace the beam so that no one will even notice. They'll think the camera eye and the microphone opening are knotholes!"

"Then the only thing we have to figure out," said Bertram, "is when we do it. Mom and Dad's office isn't that far from the living room, and Dora will also hear sawing from wherever she is."

"Well, there's only one thing to do with Dora," said Poppa. "We'll have to tell her what we're up to. She's a good sport. After all, we trusted her with the walking statue. As for Clark and Marie, don't they have to go out at all this week, for, say, two or three hours? That's all it will take at the most, to be on the safe side."

"I'll go take a look at their calendar," said Bertram. He ran upstairs and quietly opened the door to his parents' office. He quickly skimmed their calendar and then returned to the workroom. "They're having dinner with Janelle and Henry Ames the day after tomorrow," he announced. "That's when we'll do it."

Two days passed, and everything went as planned. Dora didn't need much convincing to join in the fun. Siggy got the camera mounted and hooked up the cable to Poppa's TV. To make sure it worked, they tried it out. Bertram and Dora remained in the living room, while Sigmund went downstairs with Poppa.

As soon as they got to Poppa's apartment, Poppa phoned upstairs and told Dora they were ready. Siggy flipped on the TV. There, to their great amazement and delight, stood Bertram in *his* living room, waving happily at the camera.

Then Bertram hummed a song that Poppa had sung to him since he was a little-boy.

Dora gave Bertram the message that the test was a success. Bertram grabbed her and they danced around the living room with joy.

Later, when Clark and Marie came home, Bertram was there to greet them. They were surprised and pleased, because Bertram didn't usually mark their comings and goings with much ceremony. Bertram figured that if he kept them occupied when they were walking into or leaving the living room, there would be less of a chance that they might see the camera — not that it was all that noticeable. There were only two more days left till New Year's Eve. He couldn't help grinning when he imagined what would happen that night . . .

"What's got into you?" Marie said to him. "You look like the cat who just swallowed the canary."

"Oh, nothing," Bertram said, shrugging.

— Nine —

Bertram's parents didn't notice the camera. The plan was for Bertram, Dora and Sigmund to join Poppa in his apartment for a late supper and to see the new year in watching TV. Dora had prepared plenty of extra food, so there was some of everything that Mr. and Mrs. Potter were serving to their guests upstairs: jambalaya, yam casserole, pecan pie à la mode and lots of hors d'oeuvres.

The group gathered in Poppa's living room to officially inaugurate his new TV. "And the best thing is, we get channel C and M," said Poppa to Sigmund, patting the television affectionately.

"C and M?" Siggy repeated, a bewildered look on his face.

"Yes, for Clark and Marie," said Poppa with a smile. "It's the Clark and Marie Show."

Sigmund turned on the set, and the picture of the upstairs living room appeared on the screen almost instantly.

"Where is everyone?" said Bertram impatiently.

"More important," said Poppa, "does the direction changer on the camera still work?"

Sigmund made an adjustment on a little box he held in his hand, and the camera angle upstairs shifted slightly.

"There's not too much room up there for the camera to move around, but it should be enough to get a lot of the room in," said Poppa. "Oh, look, there's Pygmalion floating by. He's the first guest. He always was early for everything. There he goes, through the wall."

Finally, Bertram's parents entered the room. Clark was wearing a black tuxedo he had rented for the occasion, and Marie had on her jade-green silk evening dress. Both of them looked more like they were dressed up to go to a charity ball in New Orleans than to eat jambalaya in their own living room.

The sound pickup was surprisingly good. Bertram clearly heard his father ask his mother if she was sure she had told everybody to come at nine-thirty.

"Of course I did," said Marie. "You saw me write it on the invitations. Stop your fretting. It's only nine twenty-five."

In about ten minutes, the group in Poppa's apartment heard the doorbell ring in the upstairs living room. In another minute, Janelle and Henry Ames walked through the doorway. They were also ridiculously overdressed. Lonnie Sue Ames was in Bertram's class at school. Even though Bertram and Lonnie Sue's parents were best friends, the two of them had hated each other since the first grade.

Bertram watched, yawning, as the two couples sat on the two facing sofas, sipping from their glasses and scarfing down hors d'oeuvres.

"I wonder when the rest of the guests will arrive," said Marie idly.

"I don't care," said Janelle. "If no one else shows up, there will be more of this delicious cracked crab for me — not to mention these luscious turnovers."

Clark, Marie, and Janelle got up to look at Clark's new tropical fish in the tank in his office. But Henry had been over to see them earlier in the week and pleaded to be allowed to stay alone with the hors d'oeuvres. "Okay," said Janelle. "But leave some for the rest of us."

The little group in Poppa's apartment watched as Pygmalion floated behind Henry Ames and waved into the camera. Henry didn't notice a thing because he was so busy feeding his face.

After a few minutes, Janelle, Clark and Marie returned.

"Didn't trust me, did you?" asked Henry.

By that time, Pygmalion had slipped through the wall into the dining room. Just then, the doorbell rang again, and Clark went to answer it. He came back with two couples this time, the Rodgerses and the LeBecs.

Then two more couples arrived. "Good, almost everyone's here!" exclaimed Bertram's mother. "Excuse me for a moment — I want to check and see how the food is doing."

Dora had prepared everything for the evening's festivities, and all Mrs. Potter had to do was make sure it was warm. But she liked to pretend that she was the cook in the house, anyway.

When she went out, Janelle said to Clark, "What does Marie mean by 'almost everyone'? I didn't think anyone was missing."

"Only the Wrights," Clark said matter-of-factly.

"The Wrights, as in Horace and Nanny?" Janelle asked in disbelief. "You *are* joking, aren't you, Clark?"

"No, actually, I'm not. I thought it was time to bury the hatchet, so I invited them."

"Well, they're not really coming, are they?" Henry asked.

Janelle and Henry had listened to enough Horace and Nanny Wright stories over the years to expect this to be the last place they would turn up.

111

Just as Marie returned to the living room, the doorbell rang again. "That must be Horace and Nanny now," she said cheerfully. "Excuse me while I let them in."

Before long even Bertram and the group in Poppa's living room could hear the familiar heavy steps of the Wrights on the ceiling above them. Then suddenly they were on camera — Nanny with her strangely colored fur coat and Horace in a horribly ugly plaid tuxedo jacket.

A hush fell over the other party guests.

"I think you know everyone here, don't you?" said Bertram's mother. "And you all know Horace and Nanny, don't you?"

None of the other guests said anything — they were too stunned. Finally, Marie said, "Let me take your coats — I mean, your coat, Nanny," when she noticed that Horace wasn't wearing one. "And then, dinner is served in the dining room."

Bertram was sorry that they hadn't set up another camera in there, but there wasn't a good place to hide one. He would have given anything for a close-up of Horace piling up his plate.

Fortunately, Horace and Nanny were the first ones through the buffet line. They took the two most comfortable chairs in the living room, which were right in front of the camera. Bertram waited for the other guests to return to

112

the living room as well, but no one seemed to be coming in. He wondered if something had happened in the other room — maybe somebody had been suddenly taken ill.

But then he realized what was wrong. No one wanted to be in the same room with Horace and Nanny. The two of them were having such a good time eating, however, that he figured they probably hadn't noticed.

But Pygmalion had! Suddenly Bertram saw him float up between the Wrights' chairs. Pygmalion placed a ghostly hand on each of their shoulders.

"P-P-Phineas P-Potter! No, wait! Y-you a-are a g-ghost!" Horace stammered. "I wasn't going crazy after all the night of the play. A real, live ghost!" Horace grabbed an arm of the chair to steady himself.

"Yes, I *am* a real, live ghost," Pygmalion informed Horace in a cold, eerie voice. "And I am not Phineas Potter — I'm Pygmalion Potter and I can make real, live trouble for you unless you promise me something. Do you hear me, Horace?"

He turned toward Nanny for support. But she had fainted. Her plate was overturned on the floor, and the remains of her food were seeping into the carpet.

Horace immediately rose from his chair, upsetting *his* plate as well. He suddenly noticed that he and his wife were the only ones in the room — besides Pygmalion. "Nanny, dearest!" he shouted. "Nanny, speak to me!"

Suddenly everyone came running in from the dining room.

"What's going on?" asked Bertram's mother. "Oh, my gosh. Nanny's passed out!"

To Bertram, watching on the TV set, for a second it looked as if Horace might try to tell Marie what had really made his wife faint. Then instead, he said, "Marie Potter, you have poisoned my wife!"

"What?" was the cry from all the guests.

"I'll have you know," said Bertram's father, rising to his wife's defense, "that my wife is not much of a cook, but she has never poisoned anybody. Besides, all this food was prepared by our housekeeper, Dora. Your wife must have fainted for another reason."

"We shouldn't just stand around, we should do something. Somebody get some cold water or smelling salts," Henry Ames suggested.

Cold water was brought from the kitchen and poured over Nanny's head. Within seconds, she began coming to.

"So much for your poisoning theory, Horace," said Mr. Potter. "If we really wanted to poison her, do you think we'd be so stupid as to do it at our own house? Even if we could claim it was accidental?"

Horace held his head in his hands.

"This wasn't as much fun as I thought it would be," Bertram whispered to Poppa.

"It's because your parents invited those horrible people," said Poppa, pointing at the Wrights on the television.

"No, I also think Pygmalion wasn't himself tonight. If we had let him just do funny tricks, it might have worked out all right," said Bertram. "But I'll lay you odds that this party is going to break up in about five minutes."

"Speaking of Pygmalion, I wonder where he got to? He isn't in camera range anymore," observed Poppa.

"You don't expect him to stay around the living room with everybody staring at the Wrights, do you?" asked Bertram. "I guess not," said Poppa. "But where could he have gone? I'd really like to talk to him."

"You're not the only one," said a voice from behind them.

"Jessie Mae!" exclaimed Poppa as he wheeled around and faced the second ghost on the premises.

— Ten —

"How did *you* get here?" said Bertram, his eyes wide. "We didn't even have a seance."

"It doesn't always take something like *that* to get one of us here. Sometimes it just depends on having a near-and-dear one pioneer the way. It leaves kind of a trail for others to follow," explained Jessie Mae. "Now, be a lamb, Phineas, and get Pygmalion for me. It's time for him to come back. It's not the same with him being away on New Year's Eve. I tolerated Christmas without him, although everybody told me I was a fool. But this is where I draw the line."

"I think you'll want to know that Pygmalion has been trying to help us out with a — a nuisance," said Poppa. "We're quite proud of him."

"Even if I made a wreck of things tonight?" said a voice. It was Pygmalion, floating through the wall of Poppa's living room.

"Oh, I suppose so," said Poppa. "You know we've had our disagreements — "

116

"What would a Potter grandfather-grandson relationship be without those?" said Pygmalion. He turned to Bertram.

"Poppa and I disagree sometimes," Bertram said, "but most of the time we don't."

"Just you wait," said Pygmalion. "I know what I'm talking about. But that doesn't mean that people can't still love each other."

"That's right," said Jessie Mae. "You and I obviously disagree on the length of time you should have stayed here without coming to get me. But I think we still love each other."

"Not to interrupt this discussion," said Dora, "but it looks like the party is breaking up."

All heads turned toward the TV screen, where a partly revived Nanny was half surrounded by the other women, who all seemed to have their coats on. Marie was saying, "Now, there's no need for everyone to leave."

"We don't want to get in the way," said Janelle. "We think you could all use some peace and quiet."

"But it isn't even midnight," Marie protested.

"There's always next year," Janelle said. "Don't worry about it. Everything will be all right."

"I'm glad she's so sure about that," said Poppa wryly. "I have an idea," said Pygmalion. "I think I can save this evening yet."

"Only if you come back with me this instant," said Jessie Mae.

"Would you deprive me of the supreme pleasure of ensuring that generations of Potters to come will be able to occupy this wonderful museum that I founded?"

Jessie Mae thought it over for a minute, then shook her head.

" *And* I'll still be able to make it make to the other side with you by midnight," promised Pygmalion. "Now, here's the plan. We wait outside for Horace and Nanny. Phineas, you and Bertram will be waiting nearby, but I'll be the one who actually intercepts them at their car."

"This sounds like fun," said Jessie Mae. "Do I know these people?"

"Do you remember Silas Wright that I've told you about? Well, this is his grandson and the grandson's wife."

Jessie Mae nodded. "I'm beginning to understand the problem," she said.

"I'd ask you along, but I think this is a one-ghost job," said Pygmalion.

"Can't I just watch from the sidelines?" said Jessie Mae.

"Okay. Now, let's go. We don't want to miss them."

So Poppa and Bertram, followed by Pygmalion and Jessie Mae, made their way across the wide front yard of the Fear Factory. They went clear across to the other side of the building, where Horace and Nanny would be coming out of the Potters' apartment.

"There's Horace now," said Bertram. "I wonder where Nanny is."

"Maybe Horace is getting the car warmed up for Nanny," said Poppa.

"It isn't that cold outside," said Bertram.

"No, but remember, she's just had a shock."

While Bertram and Poppa waited alongside the building with Jessie Mae, Pygmalion appeared next to the driver's door of Horace's car.

"Y-yes? What do you want?" asked Horace worriedly. "Go away and leave me alone."

"For that, you have to promise not to harass my grandson or his family or try to close down their business," Pygmalion said sternly.

Horace thought it over a minute. "But what will I tell the Citizens for Decency?" he asked in a shaking voice. "They look to me for moral leadership. If I tell them to lay off, they'll think I've gone soft."

"That's your decision," said Pygmalion. "But remember, I'll be watching you."

"No matter what I do, I'm sure there are some of the Citizens who will continue onward in the fight against the Fear Factory," said Horace.

"Well, if you *don't* agree to our deal, I will personally make sure that *you* get blamed for all the weird things I do around town. After all, who would believe that a ghost did them?" Pygmalion asked, chuckling.

"Oh." Horace was dumbfounded. He was used to making the threats. Now the tables were turned, and he was feeling mighty uncomfortable. "Well, I guess I don't have any choice, do I?"

"No, not much," agreed Pygmalion.

"All right, then," said Horace. "I won't try to close down the Fear Factory."

"Fine. Then I will leave," said Pygmalion.

Personally, Bertram figured that the mayor was only planning to lay off his crusade against the Fear Factory temporarily. Once Pygmalion was gone, he would resume his campaign.

Pygmalion continued, "Don't get the idea that just because we're gone, you can bother my grandson and his family again. I'm no farther away than a quick call. It's hardly more difficult to reach out and touch a ghost than it is to make a telephone call."

"Oh, all right. You win," said Horace. "Now, disappear, or whatever it is you do, before my wife comes out. I don't think her delicate system can take any more of you tonight."

Flashing a victory sign, Pygmalion floated back toward the others. "I won't say we've won the war, but at least we've won the battle. He understands that if he attacks you again, I'll show up and make life pretty uncomfortable for him."

Poppa reached out, and despite the fact that there was nothing really to hug — just the image of some clothes and a bunch of night air — he hugged his grandfather. Then he turned to Jessie Mae and hugged her, too. And for good measure, he hugged Bertram. Then the four of them went back to Poppa's apartment to tell Dora and Siggy the news.

"Pygmalion," said Jessie Mae abruptly. "If we hurry, we'll have time to get back over before the new year begins. Come, dear."

Pygmalion looked a bit regretful.

"You know you can come again," said Jessie Mae.

"That's right," said Poppa. "You know you're always welcome — even if we disagree about the museum."

"That reminds me," said Pygmalion. "We never did finish discussing that."

"Good-bye, dears," said Jessie Mae. "Thank you for taking such good care of my Pygmalion."

"Good-bye, all," said Pygmalion with a nod of his head and a tap of his cane on the wall.

With that, he and Jessie Mae floated through the wall.

"Just like that?" gasped Dora.

"I'm sad that they're gone," said Bertram. "I

121

was getting to like having a ghost around the house. Just think what he might have done for business."

"You're right," said Poppa. "I'll have to think about that."

"Since the party is over upstairs, why don't we tune in to real TV and see in the new year?" suggested Dora.

"You don't call vat I hook up *real* teevee?" asked Sigmund. He looked hurt.

No sooner had they tuned in to a dance show than they heard a banging at the door to Poppa's apartment.

Poppa quickly answered it. Bertram's mother and father were standing there, with a bottle of ginger ale and some glasses in their hands. "Happy New Year!" they shouted.

When no one said anything in return besides "Happy New Year," Marie said, "I think it's strange that no one has asked us why we're not upstairs at our party."

"Why aren't you upstairs at your party?" Bertram asked, just to humor her.

"Well, it was the worst mistake inviting Horace and Nanny. They were going on about that ghost business again. Honestly, I think they've come unglued," his mother answered, shaking her head. "Anyway, after that nobody wanted to stay, and who could blame them? Besides, it's just nice to spend New Year's Eve with your family — don't you think so, Bertram?"

Bertram smiled. He was thinking of Pygmalion, and how nice it had been to get to know his great-great-grandfather. But before he could answer, the countdown to the new year began on TV. Everyone turned to watch it.

They all cried out, "Ten—nine—eight—seven—six—five—four—three—two—one—Happy New Year!" Then they all threw their arms around one another and clinked their glasses of ginger ale in a toast.

Don't miss the next thrilling, chilling book in the Fear Factory series, when Bertram invites the town bully to the wax museum for a truly terrifying *Fright Night!*

Plug Willard is the biggest, meanest eleven-year-old in Black Bayou. He picks on all the other kids, and everybody's afraid of him. When Bertram tells Poppa what a bully Plug is, Poppa suggests that Bertram invite him to spend a night at the Fear Factory. Between them, they plan to teach him a lesson he'll never forget.

The minute Plug arrives, Poppa and Bertram set all the machinery in motion to scare him out of his wits. Everything is going according to plan — until Bertram starts chanting a spell he's found in one of Poppa's books of magic. The spell makes Plug disappear, and now it's Bertram and Poppa who are scared. If they can't figure out a way to bring Plug back, they'll be in worse trouble than ever before!